RUNNERS

Kathy Lee

Each *Seasiders* story is complete in itself – but if you enjoy this book, you may like to read the others in the series:

Liar

Joker

Winner

The same people (plus some new ones!) appear in all the books.

Scripture Union

© Kathy Lee 2000
First Published 2000

Scripture Union, 207–209 Queensway, Bletchley, Milton Keynes
MK2 2EB, England

ISBN 1 85999 356 7

British Library Cataloguing-in-Publication Data.
A catalogue record of this book is available from the British
Library.

Printed and bound in Great Britain by Cox & Wyman Ltd,
Reading.

Contents

Chapter 1

Sea view

A kid once said he thought I was lucky. He watched me come out of the lift with a bundle of dirty sheets and a bin-bag full of rubbish. As I staggered past, he said to his mum, "That boy's lucky, isn't he? He lives here all year, not just in the holidays."

Huh! Call this lucky? I wanted to say. I wanted to pile the laundry into his arms and tip the rubbish bag over his head. But I didn't because he was only little, and because he was a Piggy. A PG, I mean. A Paying Guest.

Rule number one: Be Polite to Piggies. However rude or annoying or stupid they are, Be Polite. Otherwise they won't come back next year, and nor will their friends, and the hotel will be empty, and we'll starve. I've had this drummed into me since I was about two.

My Dad and Mum run the Sea View Hotel. Sounds quite posh, you might think. Sounds like one of the big places along the sea front, with wrought-iron balconies looking out over the beach.

I suppose we do have a Sea View, but only just. From the upper floors you can see the distant horizon, with a jumble of roof-tops and chimneys blocking out any glimpse of the shore. Sometimes the Piggies complain about this. They complain about lots of things, even though they must know it's pointless. I mean, we can't move the hotel closer to the beach, can we?

Maybe they think we ought to change the name. We could call it the Chimney-pot View or the Blue Horizon, or (as one of the Piggies said when he looked at his bill) the Costa Packet. "It would have been cheaper to go to the Costa del Sol," he muttered, "*and* we might have seen the sun once or twice."

That's the trouble with Westhaven. It's great as long as the sun shines; all the Piggies sit on the beach quite happily, turning pink if they forget the sun cream, watching their Piglets build sand castles. But when the weather's bad they have to find something else to do, and everything else – the aquarium, the Leisure Pool, the bowling alley, the Pier Theatre – costs money. You can't do much in Westhaven without spending money. I don't blame the Piggies for moaning; I moan about it too. Problem is, I can't go home at the end of a fortnight – this *is* my home.

Oh, I suppose it's not so bad in some ways. There's the sea; I've always liked the sea. I like it best in winter, when huge waves crash against the sea wall, and seagulls get blown backwards, and the beach is as empty as the Polar ice shelf.

In winter, too, the hotel gets more bearable. Everything goes quiet; half the rooms are empty. Instead of families with screaming kids, we get coach parties of gossiping old ladies, or French teenagers who don't speak enough English to moan about things. Dad and Mum stop rushing about like a fast-forwarding video, and we can all relax a bit.

Winter time is when we take our own holiday; well, obviously we can't go in August. If it's been a good season we go somewhere really nice – but if it's been a good season, Mum and Dad are usually too exhausted to do much. They just want to lie beside the swimming pool, being Piggies for a change.

In winter I don't have to share a room with my little brother David. I can take my pick of the rooms on the third floor, which are hardly ever needed. My favourite is Room 18, a double with shower ensuite and views of the... er, the horizon.

In Room 18 I can keep my belongings – my computer and my war game stuff and my CDs – safely out of David's reach. (He's ten, two years younger than me, and a real pain sometimes.) In Room 18 I can actually walk around without stepping on all his bits of Lego Technic. And I can have friends over without David wanting to know what we're doing. Why are younger brothers so nosy? When *he* has a friend round, I don't pester *him* all the time.

I had fixed up Room 18 exactly how I liked it. There was even a sign on the door: JAKE'S ROOM. DO NOT ENTER. DAVID, THIS MEANS YOU! But the winter was nearly over. It would be Easter in a few weeks; we were usually full for Easter. I would have to move back into our attic flat, into the crowded bedroom which seemed to shrink as we grew.

Never mind, I told myself... enjoy Room 18 while you've got it. Why not see if Ben wants to come over?

Chapter 2

Joke of the day

I took a big letter C made of yellow card and propped it against my window. It was a kind of secret signal. My friend Ben, who lived at the opposite side of the square, would see it if he looked out of his window. It meant *Come over if you want to*. (There were other signals: a red C for *Come over at once, top priority!* An N meaning *No, you come over here for a change, you lazy so-and-so*. A black H for *Can't, I've got homework*. Plus quite a few more; I couldn't even remember what all of them meant. Why, for instance, had we felt the need for an orange Z, or a purple P?)

Nothing happened for a while. This is the only drawback to our system; it can be ages before the other person notices the signal. In which case, yes, I do realise there is such a thing as the telephone. Or even the human foot.

I sat by the window, looking down at the square. Fountain Square... another posh name which disappoints people when they actually see the place. It's a square of terraced houses, tall and narrow. That is, they were houses originally; a lot of them have been messed around, into flats or holiday lets or antique shops. Even our hotel was once three separate houses, which is why it has lots of twisting passages, blocked-off doors, and a flight of steps leading nowhere at all.

Ben's house, though, is still a normal house. It has a single doorbell, not four with different names. It looks neat and tidy; the kitchen reminds me of soup adverts on TV. Ben has two sisters, a dog and a cat. He has a Mum and Dad who have the time to take him to the cinema and watch him play football. It's all so *normal* that I really envy him.

I could see him now, crossing the square. Ben is tall and dark – taller than me, although he's nearly a year younger. Normally he has rather a solemn expression, like the Prime Minister announcing that the country is in a state of severe crisis. But don't be fooled – the serious look is all a big act.

I should warn you about him. It's sad really: he has something wrong with his brain. Most people can only remember about ten jokes, right? Ben can remember millions of them – all terrible. The storage space in his memory has normal-sized sections for Football Facts, Geography, Friends' Birthdays, or whatever. But the storage space for jokes is the size of Wembley Stadium. He knows a joke for every occasion, even funerals and car crashes. This would be okay if he just *remembered* the jokes, but he has an unfortunate need to actually *tell* them. He can't seem to stop himself – like you can't stop yourself sneezing.

It was a cold February morning; not many people were about. A woman and girl were walking along one side of the Square. I noticed them, not because they were strangers – there are always strangers in a seaside town – but because they walked so slowly and wearily.

They looked as if they'd been walking for hours, though it was only 10 a.m. The woman had a bulging suitcase; the girl had two carrier bags. She walked a step or two behind the woman, looking totally miserable.

To my surprise I saw they were heading for our front door. Surprise – because they definitely did not look like Piggies. Piggies usually come by car, coach or taxi from the station. They don't drag themselves and their luggage here on foot.

The woman came up our front steps, closely followed by Ben. The girl stayed on the pavement. After a minute she slumped down on top of the suitcase, like an old bag-lady collapsing on a bench. All I could see, from high above, was the top of her head, but something about the way she sat made me think she might be crying...

Then Ben arrived, breathless from three flights of stairs, and I forgot about the people outside.

"Go on then," I said, "tell me now and get it over with."

"Tell you what?"

"The Joke of the Day." He always has a Joke of the Day.

"Okay. What's yellow and leaps from cake to cake?"

"I give up. What *is* yellow and leaps from cake to cake?"

"Tarzipan."

Even worse than usual. I held up an imaginary score card. "Style: two points. Content: zero."

"Two points out of five?" he said hopefully.

"Two out of five hundred thousand billion. Come on, let's play Command Base. Last night I got to Level 9."

We played on the computer for a while. It's amaz-ing how quickly time can pass on a Saturday; when I looked at the clock, three hours had gone by and it was lunchtime.

"Want some lunch?" I asked Ben.

He nodded. "Hey, what's brown and white and yellow and travels at 100 miles an hour?"

I ignored him, but he told me anyway. "A train driver's egg sandwich."

"Ha ha." I stuck a large green L in the window, to tell Ben's mum he was staying for lunch, because otherwise she would worry. (Unlike my mum, who might start to worry if I was still out at 10 p.m, but otherwise wouldn't miss me – far too busy.)

Ben thinks it would be nice to have a mum like mine... I think it would be nice to have a mum like his. We've often talked about swapping houses for a day or two. Probably my parents wouldn't even notice.

They hardly noticed when we slid into the kitchen and got ourselves some lunch from the huge hotel fridge. Except that Mum shouted "Don't you dare touch those prawns, they're for tonight!" She and Dad ignored us. They were having one of their arguments.

"Well, I told her we'd give her a month's trial," said Mum. "What's wrong with that?"

Dad said, "What if she's useless? At the end of the month we'll have to look for someone else, and by then it'll be Easter, and we may not get anyone at all."

I knew what they were on about – getting a new chambermaid. A chambermaid, in case you don't know, looks after the bedrooms in a hotel. Ever since Jean, our last chambermaid, left before Christmas, we had been short-staffed. This was why I often had to help by stripping beds, emptying bins (yuk) and cleaning bathrooms (double yuk). Even David sometimes had to push a Hoover around. (He was useless at it.)

All through the winter, Mum had promised we would find somebody by Easter. We would really *need* someone by then; the hotel would be full. Now it sounded as if she'd found the person, but Dad didn't approve.

"You don't know the first thing about her," he grumbled. "And then there's the kid. She'll get in the way. Where's she going to sleep?"

"With her mother, of course. I've put a camp bed in the room for her – there's plenty of space. Anyway, she looked like a quiet little thing. Sarah promised she wouldn't be any trouble."

"Huh! Kids are always trouble," said Dad.

Mum said, "Oh Terry, if you'd seen her... she was nearly done in. Sitting on the pavement crying. Ten years old, the same as our David, and no roof over her head, and all her belongings in two carrier bags. Poor little thing, I just couldn't –"

"Look, we're trying to run a business here, not a charity. If they're homeless they ought to go to the Council. And why *are* they homeless, anyway?"

Mum lowered her voice. "Family problems, is all Sarah would say. Maybe she'll tell us more when she gets to know us better."

"All right," Dad said grudgingly. "A month's trial. But if she's no good, out she goes."

So I had been right about the woman and the girl: they weren't Piggies. They were looking for work and a place to stay. I hoped the woman would be a good worker. I was sick and tired of being a temporary chambermaid.

As for the girl, what would she be like? "Sarah promised she wouldn't be any trouble." Unfortunately, as it turned out, Sarah was wrong.

Chapter 3

The Grays

Henry was not pleased. He'd come back from his day off to find out that we had a new member of staff – and he hadn't been consulted.

Henry, our chef, has been at Sea View for twenty years; he was here long before Dad and Mum took over. Sometimes he acts as if it's *his* hotel. Even though the bedrooms are nothing to do with him, he seems to feel he should have some say in running them. He is big and stout, with a voice that can make the saucepan lids rattle on their shelves.

When Henry is in a good mood, he's fine. He'll cook sausage and chips for David and me if we don't fancy the things on the evening menu. But when Henry's in a bad mood – take cover. He actually throws things if he gets really annoyed. So far he's never thrown a knife, but there are several dents in the wall from high-speed trays and rolling-pins. On days like that I don't go near the kitchen; I make myself beans on toast on the little cooker upstairs in our flat.

The reason he's still here is that he's a good chef. You can tell just how good when Dad takes over the kitchen on Henry's day off. It's chaos! Henry can do thirty-five Full English Breakfasts on the trot, without even sweating. Dad forgets the mushrooms or burns the bacon or gets the toaster jammed or runs out of coffee. The Piggies sit there hungrily, and meanwhile their coach arrives and has to wait for ages, blocking all one side of Fountain Square.

When Henry comes back from his day off, you would think he'd go straight to his room in the hotel basement. But the first place he makes for is usually the kitchen. He looks round suspiciously, making sure Dad's left it neat and tidy. (Usually, of course, he hasn't.) Henry shakes his head and puts everything back the way it should be.

That evening, though, things had been quiet – only nine Piggies eating in. Dad seemed to have managed reasonably well, and he'd made a special effort to tidy up afterwards. Not a knife out of place, not a dirty pan to be seen.

"Hmph!" said Henry, checking around extra carefully. He almost looked disappointed.

I was making myself a sandwich, as I usually do on Dad's kitchen days. Maybe it would be a good idea to leave some crumbs on the work-top so that Henry could clear them up... he'd enjoy that.

Just then Mum came in. "This is the kitchen," she was telling someone, "oh, and here's Henry, our chef. Henry, meet Sarah Gray, the new chambermaid as from today."

Gray was a suitable name for her, I thought. Her clothes were grey and her skin had a greyish look, as if she'd been ill and wasn't really well yet. Her hair was mouse-brown. Altogether, she looked as if she wanted to fade into the background, camouflaged as an old pair of curtains.

I guessed she was about Mum's age, but they were opposites in every way. Mum loves bright colours, lots of make-up and jewellery. She's... not fat, but what Dad calls well-covered; Sarah was as thin as a piece of string. Mum loves to talk; Sarah looked quiet, shy and rather nervous. She said hello but did not smile.

Henry didn't smile either. "Living in or out?" he barked.

"In," said Mum. "I've put them in the East Attic room that Jean used to have."

"*Them?* Is there more than one?"

"Oh yes, Sarah has a daughter. She's the same age as David. That'll be nice, won't it?"

Henry frowned. "Two more mouths to feed," he muttered. "Hope she's going to be worth the trouble."

Sarah must have heard him, but she said nothing. Mum gave him a look that meant: shut up, Henry, give the woman a chance.

"Sarah's done hotel work before," Mum said. "Waitressing, too. She's quite happy to give a hand in the dining-room when we're busy."

Henry looked the woman up and down, and I knew exactly what he was thinking: Better smarten her up a bit first, then. But he didn't dare say that in front of Mum. I think Mum is the only person Henry's scared of.

Mum showed Sarah where to find milk and tea-bags for the bedrooms, then she took her upstairs. I still hadn't heard her say a word apart from "Hello". Maybe she didn't speak much English? (That would be nothing new; we've had chambermaids from every continent in the world, except maybe Antarctica.)

"*She* won't last five minutes," said Henry. "She doesn't look strong enough to lift a feather duster, and as for waitressing – well, look at her. Like death warmed up. She'll put 'em all off their food."

He began to bang saucepans about. I picked up what was left of my sandwich and slid out.

I didn't see the girl properly until next day. David and I were in the games room, playing snooker. (Snooker is another thing David's hopeless at; he insists on holding the cue as if it's a shotgun.)

In summer the games room gets taken over by Piglets, so we steer clear of it. In winter, usually, we have it all to ourselves. So I was surprised when the girl came in. She put me off my shot and I potted the cue-ball by mistake. David laughed.

"What did you go and do that for?" I said angrily.

"Do what?"

"Creep in like that."

"I'm allowed in here," she said cheekily. "Your mam said so."

"Oh, did she?"

"Yes. She said I'm welcome to use the TV in here as we haven't got one in our room, and I must say" – suddenly her voice changed and became extremely posh – "it's simply *not* what one's used to. Standards, my dear chap. Standards! Attend to it at once, please!"

Both of us stared at her, and she giggled. "Only joking."

She was small and quite pretty, I suppose, with the unusual combination of dark brown eyes and blonde hair. (The hair was probably dyed, though. It was darker at the roots.) I am good at guessing where people come from by the way they talk, but this girl's voice was a weird mixture – one minute Northern, the next almost Welsh. Maybe she had travelled around a lot.

David said, "What's your name?"

"Katie Wil- " she said, and stopped suddenly. She looked confused for a second. "I mean, Katie Gray. What's yours?"

"I'm David Thorne. That's Jake, my brother. We live here."

"I know *that*. Hey, I bet I can beat you at snooker."

"Me or him?"

"Either. Finish this frame, then I'll play the winner."

Bossy little so-and-so, I thought. I'll soon show you.

While we went on playing, she wandered restlessly around the room, then stared out the window. There wasn't much to see; the games room is in the basement, looking out on a kind of sunken yard full of dustbins.

"Westhaven's a bit of a dump, isn't it?" she said.

Although I often thought this myself, I didn't like *her* saying it. "Why come here then?" I said coldly.

"I dunno. We just stuck a pin in the map. Actually the first time we tried it we got Stoke-on-Trent, but Mam said there wouldn't be many hotels there. So we tried again and got Westhaven." She made a face.

David said, "Where were you before this?"

"Blackpool. The Rio Grande Hotel, which is about ten times the size of this. It's got a swimming pool and a sauna and a golf course. Loads of famous people stay there. I didn't want to leave, but Mam said it was time we had a change."

Just then I potted the black, beating David by about 50 points, and said, "Want a game, then?"

To my surprise, she was good at snooker. She was *very* good. She had a break of 45 and didn't even get excited.

"Ha ha! She's massacring you!" David yelled, as if that made up for all the times I'd slaughtered him. "You better look out, Katie. Jake hates losing." (Which was pretty good, coming from David. Up to about a year ago he used to cry when he lost, or get mad and stamp out of the room.)

Very soon – much sooner than usual – it was all over. Katie had won. I won't tell you the score because it was embarrassing.

"Told you I could beat you," she crowed. "*And* I'm only ten. How old are you?"

"He's twelve," David said when I didn't reply. "How did you get to be so good? You could be a champion snooker player when you grow up."

"I might," she said, and did a twirl like a dancer. "Or I might be an actress."

Yes – she was the kind of person who liked to feel that everyone was looking at her. How could she be so different from her own mother?

Something else puzzled me, too. The mother called herself Sarah Gray. The daughter had almost come out with quite a different surname – Wilson? Wilkins? Wilberforce? Then she had quickly corrected it to Gray.

Lots of people change their names. They get married, or they take a stage name, or they simply don't like the name they were born with. All perfectly legal and above board.

But then there are people with a different reason entirely. The ones who change their name because they have something to hide. That's right – the criminals.

18

Chapter 4

Change of name

Ben said, "It's probably nothing to worry about. Probably her mum got divorced, and they've gone back to using the name she had before she got married."

"Mmm... could be." Family troubles, Mum had said – that would fit. But what about the look on Katie's face when she almost said that other name? She had looked confused and nervous... scared, even.

We were on our way to school with Neddy Fields. He lives a few doors away, and the three of us normally walk to school together, although sometimes Neddy hardly says a word to Ben and me. He's not being moody – it's just that his mind is frequently on another planet. I suppose he's a bit of a loner; he likes astronomy, bird-watching, chemistry, things like that. He's skinny and red-haired and short-sighted, probably from all the reading he does. (I mean, the reading made him short-sighted – not skinny and red-haired.)

Neddy said, "Perhaps those people simply disliked the name Willoughby, or whatever, and decided to change it. Perfectly understandable. I'm not too keen on *my* name; if I was moving to another town, I'd make people call me Edward, not Neddy."

"Would you?" I said, surprised. "But you've always been Neddy."

"Not always. Only since I started at junior school. It was Darren Wheeler and his friends who started calling me Neddy, and making donkey noises whenever they saw me."

Ben said, " I never thought you minded. The name, I mean, not the donkey noises."

Neddy said, "I'm not stupid. I knew if I made a fuss, it would only encourage Darren and his mob. So I kept my mouth shut, and after a while they got bored and started on somebody else."

"But by that time you were stuck with the name," I said. "Want us to call you Edward, then? Or Ed?"

"You can try to, if you like. You'll never remember, though," he said, looking as gloomy as Eeyore.

Ben said, "Heard the one about the Scotsman called Alistair Smellie? He went to the Registry Office to change his name, and they said, 'Weel, mon, it's a fine old Scotch name, but a' the same we can quite understand ye wantin' to change it. Whit's your new name goin' tae be?' And the man said 'James Smellie'."

"Ben," I said, "that joke stinks. The accent was putrid, too."

Neddy – Edward, I mean – began to laugh helplessly. "James Smellie!" he gasped. "I like that. Tell me another one."

What a moron, I thought. But Neddy is a lot smarter than he sometimes seems to be.

Ben told us every single joke he could think of relating to names, Scotsmen, smells, bagpipes, the Loch Ness Monster, etc. etc. He finally ran out of jokes just as we arrived at school. Ben went off to his classroom, Neddy and I headed for our own.

"Seventeen," said Neddy, looking pleased. "I was counting. That's a new personal best."

"Seventeen jokes?"

He nodded. "What interests me is the way one joke appears to trigger off another one, in his mind. A kind of chain reaction process."

"Yes, well, quite intriguing I'm sure. But why do you have to study it in depth? I mean, is it relevant? Does it have Applications in Everyday Life?"

"It will, if I can figure out how to stop the process."

"Stop Ben telling jokes? Yeah! You'll earn the undying gratitude of the entire human race."

Ben is my best friend, and has been ever since he moved into Fountain Square at the age of five. But I have to admit he has one or two failings. (I wonder what he thinks *my* failings are? Hmmmm.)

The first one you already know about. The second is more minor: it's religion. He and his whole family all go to church, and he also goes to some kind of youth group on Fridays. He asked me along a few times but I always said no. It sounded about as much fun as collecting used paper tissues.

In the end, just to shut him up, I did go – once. Neddy came along too. Neither of us liked it much. Most of the evening was spent in messing around with fabric dyes, tie-dyeing T-shirts. (The end result looked as if someone had been sick all over them.) After that, somebody called Andy gave a short but incredibly boring talk, and then we went home.

"Well, that was a waste of a Friday night," I

muttered. "Thought you said there would be football?"

"There often is. You just picked the wrong night – it might be better next week," Ben said hopefully.

"No thanks."

Neddy said to Ben, "Do you really believe what that man was saying?"

"Which bit?" said Ben.

"That God knows all about you – even knows how many hairs there are on your head. That God sees everything you do. What a ridiculous idea!"

"It says in the Bible –" Ben began, but Neddy interrupted him.

"If there is a God, which is possible, I suppose – I mean, that's something that can never be proved or disproved – if there is a God, why should he care about you? He's probably got other things on his mind, such as the inner workings of the universe. How could he notice you, an insignificant member of one species on a small planet of an unimportant star?"

Ben said, "Because he's God. He knows about every species and every planet and whatever – he made them all."

I let them argue on and on. It didn't really interest me because I had decided years ago not to believe in God.

When I was little we sometimes went to visit Mum's granny in Bournemouth. She lived in this horrible, gloomy flat; there was a picture in the hallway of a staring eye with the words *Thou God seest me*. I used to find it quite scary. Was God watching when I kicked my brother around? When I stole an extra biscuit from the tin? When I secretly picked my nose?

I was about eight when the old lady died. Around

that time, I decided not to believe in God any more; I could do as I liked.

So that was all right then. Wasn't it?

I was bored. It was a Friday night, so there was no point in signalling to Ben; he would be out you-know-where. I might as well play on Future City. I was building up this computerised metropolis, enormous and highly complicated; I'd been working on it for ages.

But what had happened? My city had gone! In its place was a tiny village which a five-year-old could have designed.

"David!" I roared, charging up the stairs. "What have you done with my save on Future City?"

David gaped at me. "I haven't touched it."

"Yes you have. You've been playing on my computer again."

"I have not. I haven't been inside your smelly room for weeks. Why would I want to?"

"Well *somebody's* messed up my save. It took me weeks to build up that city and now it's gone."

"I don't even like Future City. I haven't touched it. Anyway, if you don't want people going into Room 18, you ought to keep it locked."

"What d'you mean? I do keep it locked."

"Not all the time, you don't."

It was true; I sometimes forgot. But if a stranger had got into Room 18, surely he would nick the whole computer – not sit there playing games on it. Unless of course he was just a kid... but there weren't any Piglets in residence just now. It *must* have been David, or one of his stupid little friends.

"Listen, David, if you ever touch my computer again, I'll smash up your Lego. That's a promise. Just stay out of my room, okay? And keep your friends out, too."

"It wasn't me. It wasn't! I bet I know who it could have been, though..." He lowered his voice. "That girl Katie."

I hadn't even thought of her. I mean, most of the girls I know aren't greatly interested in computers. (Or snooker either, come to that.)

I knew Katie was around all the time during the day; she didn't seem to go to school. She could easily sneak into Room 18, certain I wouldn't come back until school was over. I would have to be extra careful about locking the door.

Should I say something? But I had no proof, only suspicions. While deciding what to do, I made a huge notice to put on my door. (PRIVATE PROPERTY. TRESPASSERS WILL BE EXECUTED.) I also told Mum, but she just laughed.

"Well, if you don't keep the door locked, you've only got yourself to blame. Anyway, it doesn't sound like she did much damage."

"Mum! I spent ages on that game. Weeks. And now it's all gone and I can't get it back."

"Look, it's nothing to get worked up about. It's only a game. If you spent less time on computer games and more time on homework –"

"It's not fair! Say something, Mum! Tell her off. Talk to her mother. The kid ought to be in school, not creeping about in other people's rooms."

"I expect she will go to school," Mum said calmly, "once they know whether they're staying here or not.

Actually I hope they do stay on at the end of the month. Sarah's a good hard worker – we need her."

"Henry doesn't think so," I muttered. Henry had taken a definite dislike to Sarah; he never spoke to her unless he had to. At least *he* would be on my side.

I told him my suspicions about Katie.

"Creeping into other people's rooms, eh?" He looked alarmed. "I never did like the look of those two. Sly, that's what they are. Got something to hide, I would say."

"I'm pretty sure they gave us a false name, too."

Henry frowned. "Very dodgy. We'd better keep an eye on them. Remember that time we had the police round here?"

That had been a few months before. Very exciting. Two policemen arrested this man and woman who were using stolen credit cards. Of course, they had signed in under a false name – Salmon, the name on the stolen card. (Dad said he always knew there was something fishy about them.)

Then another time a man stayed with us for a whole month, telling people he was doing research for a book. He suddenly vanished without paying his bill, several hundred pounds' worth. The police told us he had done the same thing in half a dozen other hotels; they never caught up with him as far as I know.

So, false names are nothing unusual in a hotel. But it's usually the Piggies who tell porkies – not the staff.

Henry was right... we ought to keep a close eye on the so-called Grays.

Chapter 5

Shopping trip

"Who's she, then?" said Darren Wheeler. "Your girlfriend, Jake?"

"David's girlfriend, more like," I said.

David had let Katie borrow his roller-blades, and now she was whizzing across the Square on them. She went much faster than David ever dared to. Her blonde hair flew out behind her; there was a huge grin on her face.

It wasn't the first time David had lent her his things. When I asked him why he bothered, he said he felt sorry for her. "She's hardly got any toys of her own. She had to leave them behind in Blackpool because she couldn't carry them. It must get pretty boring just watching telly and playing snooker all day."

"And sneaking into my room," I said, "and playing on my computer."

"She doesn't do that any more. She promised not to."

"Oh, so it *was* her, then."

David looked alarmed. "Don't tell her I told you! She didn't mean to mess up your city. It was an accident."

"You actually like her, don't you?" I said. "I can't think why. She's such a show-off."

"You're only saying that because she beat you at snooker. She's okay really, when you get to know her."

She *was* a show-off, though. She turned, zoomed back and did a couple of jumps, then glanced over at us to make sure we were still watching.

I felt I had to explain her to Darren. "She's nothing to do with me. Her mum works for us, that's all."

Darren, Neddy, Ben and I were out in the Square. There's an open space in the middle where we sometimes kick a ball around. But we'd had double games at school that afternoon, so nobody had the energy.

"I'm bored," said Ben.

"Go home then," Darren said.

"If I do, Mum will make me start on my homework. Hey, have you heard this one? Mummy, Mummy, I don't *want* to go to America... Oh shut up, and keep swimming."

Dead silence greeted this, but it didn't put him off. "Mummy, Mummy, why am I walking round in circles?... Shut up, or I'll nail your other foot to the floor."

"Sick," I said, but Darren liked it. He has a violent streak about a mile wide. I don't like Darren much; he's a trouble-maker. He lives on the corner of Fountain Square and Pump Street, in a flat above the Corner Café. Sometimes he hangs around in the Square, but more often he goes about with the Pump Street gang – Loz and Barn and Macaulay – who are also trouble in various ways.

Now he took out a packet of cigarettes (see what I mean?) and offered it around. Nobody took one.

"Are you mad?" I said. "Even if I wanted to smoke, which I don't, I wouldn't do it right here under our windows."

"Suit yourself," he said, and lit up. He was showing off really, just like Katie.

"What if your Dad sees you?" said Ben.

"Don't care if he does. He smokes forty a day himself."

"Won't he notice that you've nicked his fags?"

Darren said disdainfully, "I didn't nick these, I bought them."

"How?" said Neddy. "You're not old enough."

"Ah. There's this shop I know about, see? Old girl that runs it never asks questions. Never notices, either, if you go out with a few things you didn't pay for. She's so short-sighted she can't hardly see past the end of the till."

"Where *is* this?" said Neddy.

"Not telling. If too many people get to know about it, they'll spoil it."

After a while, though, he couldn't resist telling us more. "It's that old corner shop at the top end of Hill Street. Want to see it?"

"Okay," said Neddy, and Ben and I followed because we had nothing else to do. It was starting to get dark; street lights were coming on. When we reached it, the little corner shop was brightly lit like a stage, with us, the audience, unseen in the darkness outside. An old woman sat by the till, knitting slowly.

"There she is, see?" said Darren. "All on her lonesome. Couldn't be better. Anyone got any money? Okay, Jake, you buy a bag of crisps or something."

"Why? I don't want a bag of crisps."

"Bar of chocolate, then. Anything – go on. Ben and Neddy, you wait here."

He pushed me into the shop, which had a sign on the

door: NOT MORE THAN TWO CHILDREN AT A TIME, PLEASE. While I was paying for my Yorkie bar, he walked around the shop, but the old lady hardly glanced at him. We went out again.

When we were round the corner, Darren produced a big bottle of Coke from his jacket. "See? Like taking candy off a baby."

I realised I had just taken part in a theft. Accomplice – that was the word, wasn't it? For a moment I felt guilty... but after all, it wasn't much. Only a bottle of Coke.

Darren handed it round, looking pleased with himself. We all had a swig except Ben.

"Not keen on Coke? I'll go back and get some Fanta, if you like."

"No, don't bother," said Ben.

Neddy said, "Ben wouldn't want to drink stolen property. It's against the Ten Commandments, isn't it, Ben? *You shall not steal.* Ben thinks God's watching us all at this very moment."

Ben looked most uncomfortable, and Darren laughed. "Oops, sorry, God. I don't know how it happened. The bottle just sort of fell off the shelf. Take it back now, shall I?" He held the half-empty bottle up towards the sky and pretended to listen. "No, it's all right, I don't think God noticed us. Not this time."

"Now it's my turn," said Neddy. "Who's going to distract the old lady's attention?"

"Not me," said Ben.

"Me neither," I said. "She'll think it's strange if I go back so soon."

"Naw, she won't notice. Blind as a bat, she is. I'll do it if you like," said Darren. He seemed to be enjoying himself.

"I'm going home," said Ben suddenly. "You coming, Jake?"

"Okay. See you later, guys."

Ben looked really miserable as we walked down the hill. Miserable and guilty.

"What's the matter?" I said. "Look, you didn't do anything wrong, so what are you worried about?"

"I dunno. Maybe I should have tried to stop him..."

"How exactly? It would take a two-ton truck to stop Darren – you know what he's like."

"Yeah." All at once he began to grin. "Hey, where would you find an Irish shoplifter?"

"Don't tell me, don't tell me. Squashed under Sainsbury's."

Out of the darkness came the sound of running feet. Darren and Neddy came charging down the hill.

"Quick! Get out of here!" Darren gasped. "Come *on*!"

When we were safely back in the Square, I said, "What happened? Did she spot you?"

"*She* didn't," said Neddy, "but the camera did. One of those CCTV cameras. I was just putting my hand out for a bottle of lemonade when I looked up and saw it. Quite cunningly hidden, it was – in a corner above the magazine racks. You'd never know it was there."

Ben said, "You didn't actually nick anything, I hope."

"Of course not."

"So why the panic?" I asked. "You haven't broken any law."

"True," said Neddy. "But what about earlier? Jake and Darren, your little shopping trip would have been on camera too. I hope you were smiling."

Chapter 6

Caught on camera

I lay awake for ages that night, thinking about what might happen. (HOTEL MANAGER'S SON CAUGHT SHOPLIFTING, it would say in the local paper, and Dad would go crazy.)

In the morning things didn't seem quite so bad. As we walked to school, I said, "Even if we *were* caught on camera, does it matter? Maybe nobody was watching the camera. The old woman wasn't, I know that."

Neddy said nothing; he was in one of his silent moods. Ben said, "Some of those cameras record onto a video. So even if no one was watching at the time, they can play the tape back later. You know, like on TV crime programmes."

"Okay, but if they do that, all they'll have is our faces on film. They won't be able to track us down from that, will they? I mean, it's not like we're known to the police."

"Darren is," said Ben. "Remember when him and Loz got caught nicking off stalls in the market?"

"Oh." My heart sank. If Darren got into trouble, he wouldn't hesitate to drop me in it too.

After a long silence, Neddy said, "There's

something you should know, but you have to promise not to tell Darren."

"Okay."

"There wasn't any camera. I made it all up."

"You what?" I stared at him.

"There wasn't any camera. At least, not as far as I could see. I just wanted to give Darren a scare, and make him leave that old woman alone." He took off his glasses and rubbed them. "Darren kept on and on about how she was short-sighted, half blind. Us short-sighted people should take care of one another, don't you agree?"

Ben began to laugh. "Neddy!" I said furiously. "You just about gave me a nervous breakdown. I'll *kill* you." (HOTEL MANAGER'S SON ACCUSED OF MURDER.)

"Don't tell Darren," said Neddy. "Let him sweat for a while, and perhaps he'll start to realise that Crime Does Not Pay. Or at least he'll choose a different shop."

"You might have told *me*, though," I said, still fuming.

Ben said to Neddy, "So you never really planned on nicking anything in the first place." He sounded relieved.

"True. Does that mean you approve of what I did?"

Ben nodded.

"That's odd, because I broke another of your Ten Commandments, didn't I? The one about not telling lies."

"Yeah, I suppose so..." Ben looked as confused as I must have done two minutes earlier. (Neddy has that effect on people.)

"So if God was watching, he wouldn't be too pleased with me, right? *If* he was watching. But that's the big question, isn't it?"

"God must have several million CCTV cameras all over the place," I said. "They're well hidden, though, you have to admit."

Neddy ignored me. "It's quite logical to believe in some kind of... of creative Life Force. Something created the universe. Something keeps it all going. If people want to call that God, then fine. But why should it be interested in us? That's the illogical part."

Ben said, "God *is* interested. He cares about us, he listens to us. It says in the Bible –"

"Oh, then it *must* be true," said Neddy sarcastically, "if it says so in the *Bible*."

Ben was no match for Neddy in an argument. I knew what he would do – what he always did when at a loss for words: start telling jokes.

"Shut up, Neddy," I said. "It's a free country. Ben can believe whatever he wants to. What's it matter to you?"

That's the trouble with Neddy. Most of the time he's okay, but sometimes... well, he sort of turns on people. And he doesn't understand why they don't like it.

In March we had an amazing week, warm and sunny. It was more like June.

"Global warming," said Neddy. "People ought to be worried, not pleased."

"Well, my dad's pleased," I said. "We've got loads of last-minute bookings."

Mum and Sarah were scurrying around, opening up

the third-floor rooms which had been unused all winter. Any minute now, Mum would remember about Room 18 and make me start moving my things out.

"Jake!" Mum shouted, and I answered reluctantly.

"Do me a favour – take David down to the beach with his boat. He keeps on and on about it, but I haven't had a minute to spare today."

"All right. As long as he lets me have a go of it." The boat was a remote-controlled speed-boat, David's best Christmas present, which had never yet been for a trial run – the weather had been too bad.

"Great! Thanks, Jake!" said David. "Can Katie come too?"

"No," I said.

"Oh yes, take Katie," Mum said. "Get her out for a change. She's hardly seen the sea yet."

We set off, with Katie rushing ahead and back, exactly like an excited puppy.

"Why did Mum say that?" I asked David. "About Katie getting out for a change?"

"She never seems to go out much," he said. "Her mum stays indoors most of the time even when she's not working. And Katie's not allowed out on her own, except in the Square where her mum can keep an eye on her. She gets fed up with it sometimes."

It was a beautiful day; people were strolling along the pier, sun-bathing, buying ice-creams and postcards... all the things that Piggies do all summer long, though it wasn't even Easter yet. The only thing they weren't doing was swimming. The sea was as calm as a paddling-pool, and little ripples licked gently at the sand, tempting people to dip their toes in. But even the bravest soon came out again. The water was *freezing*.

The empty sea was ideal for trying out David's boat. It went really well. At top speed it could aquaplane just like a real racing boat. Half a dozen kids gathered round to watch, asking for a turn at the controls, but David wouldn't let anyone have a go except himself and Katie and me. "They'll let it go too far out," he said.

"Yeah. This isn't a boating lake," I said. "If the steering got jammed, the boat could end up in France."

"Look this way, kids! Big smile now!"

It was a man with a camera. I recognised him – the photographer from the *Westhaven Weekly*. He was always around at school fêtes and special events; the warm weather, I suppose, was a sort of special event too.

Katie, who had the controls of the boat, turned to face the camera. She started to smile that big smile of hers – but then her face changed. She shoved the control panel back into David's hand and turned her back on all of us.

It was so unlike her usual behaviour. (If David had been the one refusing to be photographed, I'd hardly have noticed. We've got dozens of holiday snaps showing Mum and me, or Dad and me, grinning away next to the back of David's head.) The camera clicked away, but Katie didn't turn round once. She just stared glumly out at the sea until the photographer went away.

It was my turn at the controls. I made the boat sweep out in a wide arc... but something was wrong. It was slowing down, losing power... oh no! The batteries must have run out!

Frantically I turned the controls, heading the boat

back towards us. But the engine was totally silent now. The boat glided on for a few metres, then came to a stop, gently bobbing on the slow, smooth waves.

"Jake!" David cried. "I told you not to let it go out too far!"

"Oh, shut up. I can get it back – the water's not that deep." It would be cold, though. I hesitated, wondering which would be worse – taking my jeans off and going out there in my underpants, or walking back home in soaking wet jeans. Wet jeans, I decided, would be worse, and I started taking them off.

"Katie – come back!" David yelled. I looked round. Katie was already paddling out, giving little shrieks as the ice-cold water climbed from her ankles towards her knees. It was okay for her; she had a skirt on.

"Katie, don't be daft," I called, but by now she was more than half-way there. Deeper and deeper – the water licked at the hem of her skirt, then soaked it completely. She still cried out at the coldness of it, but went on bravely without stopping. You had to admire her, really.

She made it to the boat. The water was up to her waist by now, but she turned and gave us a triumphant smile. Everybody started clapping and cheering.

Click! Click! The photographer was back. "Smile for me again, sweetheart," he called out.

"No!" she cried. "No photos. Go away!" Shielding her face with one hand, she began to wade back to the beach.

"Who does she think she is – Garbo?" the photographer muttered. But he didn't hang around. He went off towards the pier, snapping at people as he went. (With his camera, I mean, not his teeth.)

Katie was shivering violently; she was soaked from the waist down. A Piggy mum lent her a towel to rub her legs dry, but she had no other clothes to change into.

"Come on," I said, "better get you back home. Can you run? It'll warm you up a bit."

"Y-y-yes. But don't tell M-M-Mam about the f-f-f-photos, or she'll go m-m-mad."

I wondered why... but it didn't seem the right time to ask. We hurried Katie back to Sea View (TEN MINUTES' WALK FROM BEACH) in about three minutes flat. Her mum was quite upset at the state she was in; I got the feeling it would be a long time before Katie was allowed out with us again.

However, she didn't catch pneumonia or anything. She was fine after a hot bath. But for the next few days she went around looking slightly anxious. On Thursday, when the *Westhaven Weekly* arrived, she carted it off to the games room and looked through it carefully.

"Looking for your photo?" David asked her.

"It's all right," she said, "it isn't there."

"Why don't you want your picture in the paper?" I asked.

"Why don't you mind your own business?" She went out, slamming the door.

So I didn't tell her what I'd seen in school that afternoon. It was in a three-day-old copy of the *Daily Mirror,* which I was laying out on tables in the Art Room. PHEW, WHAT A SCORCHER! said the headline above three big photos. Girls in bikinis at Brighton, old ladies in deck-chairs at Eastbourne... and Katie in the sea.

It was a good photo: sunlight glinting on the water, and Katie's smile, even brighter than the sun, as she held David's boat aloft. This must have been before she realised the photographer was there. "Come on in, the water's lovely at Westhaven," the caption read.

Should I tell her or not? In the end I decided not to mention it. The thing had already happened; it couldn't be prevented. Knowing about it would only upset her and get her into trouble with her mum.

But why, why on earth should her mum disapprove? Most parents would be quite proud to see their child's picture in the paper. It didn't make sense...

Chapter 7

Ask me no questions

"Katie must be a vampire," said Darren.

"You what?"

"A vampire or a ghost or something, that won't show up in photos. And she doesn't want anybody to know."

"Mummy, Mummy, what's a vampire?" said Ben. "...Shut up and drink your soup before it clots."

"Don't talk stupid," I said to both of them. "She does show up in photos – look at this." I had torn out the photo from the paper, meaning at the time to give it to Katie. "It was in the *Daily Mirror* on Monday, but she doesn't know. Don't tell her."

"Interesting," said Neddy. "Of course, there are other reasons why people avoid being photographed."

"Such as?"

He said, "Such as famous people who don't want to be mobbed by thousands of adoring fans."

"Yeah, well Katie isn't famous." Although she would probably like to be, one day.

"Okay, discard that theory," Neddy said. "Here's another one: they're hiding from somebody."

"Yes!" I said. "That would be why Sarah hardly

ever goes out. She doesn't let Katie out much either – not even to go to school."

"Isn't that illegal?" said Ben. "*Everybody* has to go to school."

Darren said, "So who are they hiding from – the Bill?"

"Oh sure," I said, "like Katie's mum robbed a bank or something. Looks the type, doesn't she?"

"She could be a poisoner," said Darren hopefully, "or a kidnapper or a thief."

A thief? It takes one to know one, I nearly said.

"It might not be the police she's hiding from," said Ben. "Maybe it's somebody they owe money to."

"Maybe it's Katie's cruel father who used to beat her," said Neddy. "Does she ever mention a father?"

"No... she never talks about the past much at all. The only thing I know is, they left Blackpool in a hurry. Stuck a pin in the map to decide where they were going, and looked for work when they got here."

"Left in a hurry – yeah. It does sound like they're on the run," said Ben.

"And now," said Neddy, one step ahead of us as usual, "Katie's picture has been in newspapers all up and down the country. I wonder if anyone's spotted her?"

Friday night, and I was up in my room, which wouldn't be mine much longer. Mum said I had to be out before next weekend so I might as well begin sorting out my things. It was a mammoth task. It's weird how magazines and socks and CD cases can worm their way under the furniture, like little mice looking for a place to hide.

Getting bored, I wandered down to the games room, but the snooker table was already in use; Katie was trying to teach David a complicated trick shot.

"Don't bother," I said, "he'll never get the hang of it. Good trick, though. Where did you learn that?"

"Scarborough," she said.

"Scarborough? I thought you used to live in Blackpool."

"Scarborough was before Blackpool," she said. "Look David, if you aim just there, down and to the left —"

David took the shot and missed. Patiently she set the balls in line again.

"And where were you before that?" I asked.

"Prestatyn. Or was it Margate? I get mixed up."

"You *have* moved around a bit," I said. "What about school?"

"What about it?"

"Wasn't it a pain, changing schools every time you moved?"

"Katie hasn't been to school for ages," said David enviously. "Her mum teaches her when she's not at work."

Katie said, "I did go to school in Prestatyn, but that was before..." Her voice trailed off and stopped.

"Before what?"

"Never you mind." And then she said something rather odd. "Ask me no questions, I'll tell you no lies. That's what Mam always says."

I spent ages moving my things out of Room 18 and up the narrow stairs to our flat. It's in the attic, which would have been the servants' area when the house was originally built. All the rooms are awkward shapes, with walls that slope inwards like the sides of a tent.

It was terrible having to share a bedroom again – and not a big bedroom, either. David had kindly moved all his junk off my bed and piled it in heaps on the floor. Some of my stuff had to go on the floor, too. We were waiting for Dad to put up some more shelves, which he'd promised to do about a year ago, "when I have a spare minute".

I would have to get used to David's snoring all over again, after a winter of silence. I wouldn't be able to use my TV or my computer when David had gone to bed. It was so unfair!

"It's even worse for Katie," said David. "She's got to sleep on a camp bed in her mum's room."

"I thought Mum was going to sort out the East Attic box-room so Katie could have her own room." Mum and Dad had talked about this, when they agreed Sarah could stay on at the end of her trial month.

"Of *course* we're keeping her on," Mum had said. "She's very efficient. Never says much, just gets on with the work. What have you got against her?"

"Nothing really," said Dad, "except that she is so secretive. And Henry doesn't get on with her. He's always moaning about her; it makes for a bad atmosphere."

"Oh well, you know what Henry's like," said Mum. "He'll come round in the end." And she went on about keeping Sarah happy so that she would stay on with us through the summer. That was when she had the idea about making a bedroom for Katie.

"But Sarah said no," David told me. "She wants

42

Katie to go on sleeping in the same room as her."

"Why? I mean Katie's not a baby."

"Sarah told Mum it's because Katie has nightmares – but it isn't true. *Sarah's* the one who has nightmares. She talks in her sleep and even screams out loud, sometimes. Then Katie has to wake her up and tell her it's only a dream."

This was news to me. "What does she dream about – does Katie know?"

"Somebody coming to get her. To kill her."

"How weird," I said. "And is it true?"

"Is what true?"

"That somebody wants to kill her."

"Of course not," said David scornfully. "I told you – it's only a dream."

Chapter 8

In training

"Are you going in for this Fun Run thing, Jake?" said Ben's mum.

"Not sure," I said cautiously. "I don't mind the running, but I'm not so keen on going round getting people to sponsor me."

Ben said, "I've got the opposite problem. Loads of sponsors, but I don't know if I can run five miles. I've never tried."

"How did you find loads of sponsors?"

"At church. They all said what a good cause it is, and put down vast amounts of money. So what will happen if I collapse in a heap after the first half-mile?"

"You'll look an idiot, that's what will happen," I said.

Our school was organising a Fun Run in aid of famine victims in Africa. Taking part was entirely optional, the Head kept saying. However, all runners would be invited to an end-of-term party, and – most important – they'd each get a certificate personally signed by the Head. Wow!

"Is it worth it?" said Ben gloomily.

His mum said, "Of course it is. Just think, the

money you'll make could save a life. Several lives, probably."

"You ought to get in training," I said. "I'll help if you like – I'll be your personal trainer."

I am in the school cross-country team, which came fourth out of the whole county last year. The only running Ben ever does is on a football pitch.

"Slow *down*, Ben," I kept saying on our first training run.

After about a mile he slowed down all right – to a stop. "See? It's hopeless," he panted.

"Only because you started off too fast. You've got to pace yourself – it's not a sprint. It's not even a race. You only need to make sure you cover the distance, okay?"

The second day was better, and the third day we made it half-way around the Basin before he ground to a halt. The Basin is a huge salt-water lake inland from the town. (I mean, at high tide it's a lake; at low tide it's just mud flats, where careless Piggies run boats aground and get stuck until the next high tide.) The rumour was that the Fun Run course would be a complete circuit of the Basin, starting and finishing at the harbour bridge.

"I hope they're right about that," Ben gasped. "At least it will all be on the flat."

It was certainly very flat where we were standing. Flat and empty. Southwards, a marshy field stretched out to the reed-beds at the edge of the Basin. Northwards, more marshy fields, with the river looping through them in long, slow curves. We were on a country road which had very little traffic, and absolutely no buses. The only way home was on our own two feet; at this rate it would be dark before we got there.

"Oh, my legs," Ben moaned like an old granny. "If we see a phone-box I'm going to ring my mum to come and pick us up."

"Fine." I knew it was no good phoning *my* mum – she'd be far too busy.

But there were no phone boxes; hardly even any buildings on that lonely road. A cottage which we saw from a long way off turned out, as we approached, to be a ruin. The town, far away across the Basin, seemed to be getting no closer as we trudged on.

We came to a gateway where a bike was propped up against the fence. "Funny place to leave a bike," I said. "Where's the owner?"

Ben said, "It looks a bit like Neddy's bike. Hey, it *is* Neddy's! How weird."

We looked around. Apart from a few sea birds, nothing moved in that grey, empty landscape.

"He's been abducted by aliens," I said, "or got sucked down into the marsh." I didn't believe it really, but all the same I felt a chill creeping over my body. Where on earth was he?

"Neddy!" Ben shouted. "Neddy! Are you there?"

No answer.

"Where do you think he went? Into that field?"

We went through the gateway and across the field, shouting his name. On the far side of the field, beyond a belt of tall reeds, the brown mud-flats of the Basin stretched out into the distance. There was quicksand out there; now and then, idiotic Piggies had to watch their vehicles being swallowed up in it. But Neddy knew about the danger, surely?

"Neddy!" I yelled. "If you can hear us, shout!" A great cloud of birds arose on clattering wings.

And quite suddenly he was there – right next to us. "Do you *have* to make so much noise? You're scaring every living creature within a five-mile radius."

"Oh! But we saw your bike – we thought –"

"Where on earth *were* you?"

"In the hide, of course. Over there."

Beyond the tall reeds, I could just make out a low brown building, like an unwanted garden shed which had been dumped at the high-tide mark. A narrow pathway led through the reeds, with wooden duckboards to stop you sinking into the mud.

"I never noticed it," I said.

"Well, that *is* rather the idea of a hide," said Neddy. "Want to go in?"

It really was just a shed, with a bench to sit on and horizontal slits for windows. Neddy let us try out his binoculars, pointing out various birds – redshanks and curlews and godwits – which all looked very similar to me. (The only birds I can name accurately are robins and ostriches.)

"How long have you been sitting here?" I asked.

"An hour or so, probably."

"Don't you get bored?"

"No. Don't *you* get bored, jogging along mindlessly, hardly noticing the countryside?"

"Who says we don't notice things?" I said. "We've already seen two hedgehogs and a rabbit."

"Yeah," said Ben. "*And* we didn't need a hut to observe them from –"

"Seeing as they were squashed flat on the road," I explained.

"Why did the rabbit cross the road?" said Ben. "To show his girlfriend he had guts."

"Get out," said Neddy. "Just get out, you philistines."

We trudged back across the field. As we got to the gate, a battered-looking white van came to a stop just beside it, and Macaulay Burton got out of the passenger side. Macaulay is one of the Pump Street mob – who can often mean trouble, as I said before. He's only a year older than us but he looks about sixteen.

"This your bike?" he said.

"No, Neddy's."

"Oh. Think he'd miss it?"

"Yeah – and anyway it's chained to the fence," I said.

"No problem," said Macaulay. "Harrison's got a saw in the back." Harrison is Macaulay's big brother; he was driving the van. (It had a sign on the bumper: *Do not wash. This vehicle is taking part in a scientific dirt test.*)

Ben and I stood in front of the bike, ready to defend it. But Harrison said in a weary voice, "Leave it, Cauli. How many times have I told you, don't mess on your own doorstep?" I suppose he meant, don't nick things off neighbours – not in front of witnesses, anyway. "You kids want a lift back into town?" he asked unexpectedly.

Ben and I looked at each other. We were not allowed to take lifts off strangers, but Macaulay wasn't a stranger, was he? And we had been out a long time. Ben's mum must be wondering where we were.

We got into the back of the van, on top of what looked like a heap of scaffolding. It rattled alarmingly as the van picked up speed. The van had no windows in its sides, and the glass in the back doors had been painted over. After a while, unable to see out, I began to feel quite car-sick, or should that be van-sick?

"What you doing out here?" Macaulay yelled over his shoulder. "Practising for the Fun Run?"

"Yeah."

"So are we. Checking out the route, I mean."

"Oh," I said, trying not to show my amazement. "Are you going in for it, then?"

"Dead right I am. And so are Loz and Barn."

Even more amazing. Barn got his name, not only because it was short for Barnabas, but because he was built like the side of a house. I couldn't imagine him completing a five-mile run. Plus Loz and Barn and Macaulay had never before shown any concern for famine victims.

They dropped us off in Fountain Square. "Thanks!" I shouted as the van roared away.

Ben said, "Why did they do that? To get us out of the way, so they can nip back and pick up Neddy's bike?"

"He should be on his way home by now," I said. "It's nearly dark. But we'd better warn him to hide it next time."

"Another thing – why are that lot going in for the Fun Run?"

"No idea. Must be because they're dying to have their own personal certificate, signed by the Head."

Chapter 9

Confidential

In the end I decided to do the Fun Run too, mainly to keep Ben company. I only had about six sponsors (including Katie, who sponsored me for 20p a mile, which was generous of her – I knew she didn't get much pocket money.) Ben had gone on to his fourth sponsor form; if he finished the course, he would raise more than two hundred quid.

"Yeah," he said, "*if*."

"We'll do it, no problem," I said. "The only thing that could defeat us now would be really bad weather."

"Or a broken leg," Neddy put in helpfully. (Neddy was not going to run but had volunteered to be a steward.)

"Or an attack by killer seagulls," I said.

"Or a tidal wave."

"Or Barn falling over and blocking the road. By the way, I haven't seen any of the Pump Street lot out training, have *you*?"

By now there were quite a lot of people jogging around Westhaven each evening. One of them was Mr Wild, the games teacher, who planned to do the run in a polar bear outfit. (What do polar bears have to do with Africa? Very little. What do games teachers know about Geography? Even less.)

There was just over a week to go. "Tomorrow's Saturday..." I began.

"That's not surprising," said Neddy, "in view of the fact that it's Friday today."

"I meant, that gives us time to do a really long run."

"Okay," said Ben. "You coming to Club tonight, Neddy?"

"Possibly. I haven't decided yet."

"You're not still going to that youth club place, are you?" I said to Neddy.

"I have been along once or twice, yes," he said.

"Better be careful, or they'll turn you into a Christian! You don't believe in God and all that, though. Do you?"

"Not the God that Christians talk about, no. I do think something must have created the universe, though. It's far too amazing and intricate to have happened by chance... Something made it."

"Somebody, you mean," said Ben.

Neddy said, "That's where Christians get it so wrong. They keep talking about God as if he's a person – like their next-door neighbour. They think they can speak to him and he'll actually listen."

"God does listen to us," said Ben.

"Oh yeah?" I said. "Then why is there still a famine in Africa? I bet loads of people have prayed about that."

"Well... God doesn't always give us what we ask for. But a lot of the time, he does. He does listen."

"Give us an example," said Neddy.

Ben said, "Last week, I couldn't find my maths

homework book and I knew I'd get in big trouble. I looked everywhere – Mum did, too. We still couldn't find it. So then we prayed about it – and Mum got this idea suddenly, to look down the side of the sofa. And there it was."

Neddy said, "And you actually think that was an answer to prayer? Don't be ridiculous. If God exists, why would he care about you and your maths homework? Christians are like ants imagining they can communicate with an elephant. 'Oh no, don't step on us, please!' they say in ant language, and if the elephant passes by without stepping on them, they tell each other, 'See? Prayer really works.' But the elephant didn't even notice they were there."

I laughed. Answer that one, Ben!

"Wait a minute," said Ben. "There is a way an elephant could communicate with an ant. What is it?"

"I give up. How can an elephant talk to an ant?" I said, waiting for the punchline.

"The elephant," he said, "could turn into an ant. Then they'd be able to communicate, right?"

"Let me know when I'm supposed to laugh," I said.

But Neddy said thoughtfully, "You mean, God could turn himself into a man. How?"

"I don't know how. I just know it's already happened – when Jesus was on earth."

Neddy, for once, looked taken aback. "Well, yes," he said. "I suppose that is a point of view."

By now I was bored with this. I told one of the few jokes I can ever remember. "Why is an elephant large, grey and wrinkled? ...Because if it was small, white and smooth it would be an aspirin."

Both of them glared at me. "Time I was going," I said.

On the Saturday, I'd planned to go running with Ben, but it never happened. I had to help out because Sarah was ill in bed.

"What's the matter with her?" said Dad, cross because it was a Saturday and we were busy.

"She's feverish and she keeps being sick," said Mum. "She looks absolutely awful."

"I expect Henry poisoned her," I whispered to David.

"Right then, all hands on deck," Mum ordered. "I'll start on the bedrooms as soon as I finish serving breakfast. Boys, you can clear the tables and then come upstairs to help."

This always happens if someone's off sick or on holiday. You get a bit of extra pocket money – not enough, though, to make up for having your Saturday ruined.

David and I started clearing the breakfast tables at top speed, whipping the plates from under the noses of startled Piggies. Come on, hurry up! Get your heads out of the trough! We also had to keep an eye on Reception; Mum was upstairs and Dad had gone to the fish market. If someone wanted to pay his bill I would need to call Mum, but most other things I could handle.

Ping! Someone had pressed the bell that said *Ring for Attention*. I hurried out into the hall. It was a woman; I didn't recognise her as one of our Piggies, but then she had the sort of face that you don't notice particularly. Pleasant, ordinary, middle-aged.

"Can I help you?" I said.

She looked at me rather doubtfully. "I'd like to speak to the manager, please."

"I'm afraid he's out. You could leave a message if you like or call back in an hour or so."

"Well, perhaps you can help me then. I'm trying to trace this woman; I believe she was in Westhaven a couple of weeks ago. Have you seen her?"

I glanced at the photo, which showed a pretty woman with dark curly hair, smiling at the camera.

"No, I don't think so," I said. "What's her name?"

"Jane Martin, but she's probably using a different name at the moment."

"Is she a criminal, then? Are you from the police?"

"Not police, no. I'm a private detective."

I must have looked as surprised as I felt. She wasn't at all like the detectives on TV. Did she carry a gun in her handbag? Could she kick a door in with her neatly-polished shoes?

She smiled, as if guessing my thoughts. "I specialise in tracing people who go missing. As far as I know this lady isn't a criminal, but my client is anxious to find her."

"Why?"

"I'm sorry, that's confidential – I'm not allowed to discuss it. By the way, the photograph is quite old; she may look rather different now. But here's a more recent picture of her young daughter." And she held out another photo.

It was one I knew quite well. I had seen it last in the *Daily Mirror*...

I looked again at the first photo. Yes, it could just possibly be Sarah – much younger, with a different hairstyle and a smile. (I had never once seen Sarah smiling.)

My mind was racing. Surely this woman couldn't be the person that Sarah was afraid of – the one who was coming to get her, to kill her. She looked as if she'd have trouble killing a spider, never mind a human being.

All the same, someone had sent the woman out to look for Sarah. *My client is anxious to find her...*

"You recognise the girl, don't you?" the detective said.

It was no use pretending. "Yes... I have seen her. It was on the beach. That's my brother's boat she's holding in the photo."

"Is it really? When was this?"

"The Saturday before last – that hot weekend."

"And have you any idea where she is now?"

"No." The lies came easily off my tongue. "We saw her on the beach, that's all. She went into the water and got David's boat out. I don't know where she went after that."

Was I doing the right thing, or was I being stupid? Perhaps the mysterious client meant good and not harm – perhaps someone had died and left Sarah a fortune. Oh, help...

"You're absolutely certain?" the detective said. "You only saw her that one time?"

I nodded.

"And you didn't see who she was with?"

"I didn't really notice."

She sighed. "Well, if you see her again, will you give me a ring? Here's my business card. You never know, my client may be prepared to give a reward to the person who finds her." She looked at a printed list of hotels and ticked off Sea View. "Nine down, thirty-three to go," she said, and sighed again.

Just then, David pushed a rattling trolley of plates out of the dining-room.

"Goodness," the woman said, "is this entire hotel run by children?"

"More or less," I said. "You just can't get the staff these days."

She laughed and went out. I looked at the card she'd given me: *Irene Stuart, Private Investigator. Confidential and Discreet. Matrimonial & Adoption Enquiries. Missing Persons Traced.*

"What was all that about?" asked David.

I turned the card over and over in my hand. "I only wish I knew."

Chapter 10

Move on again

The thing to do, I decided, was talk to Katie. If I told Sarah that someone was looking for her all over Westhaven, she would do what she'd done before: pack up her things and make a run for it. In which case I might have helped a criminal to escape.

But the detective had said she wasn't looking for a criminal... as far as she knew. If Sarah had done nothing wrong, then shouldn't I warn her that an enemy was looking for her? If it *was* an enemy...

My thoughts went round and round endlessly; like the endless trek from room to room, emptying bins and ashtrays, removing dirty towels, cleaning baths... all the jobs that would need to be done again tomorrow and the day after, endlessly... If Sarah left, it might be weeks before we got someone else to take over. I really didn't want her to leave.

Katie was helping us with the bedrooms; she knew the routine exactly without being told. "I often help Mam when I'm bored," she said, as we changed the king-size bed in Room 3. "It gives me something to do."

"I thought you would be starting school, now

you've got settled here," I said.

She shook her head. "Mam doesn't want me to. She says it's safer not to."

Now was my chance. "Er... is it true that your mum thinks somebody –"

The door opened. My mouth closed.

But it was only Mum, bustling in with the Hoover. "Finished in here? Good. Eleven and Twelve have both checked out, so you can do them next."

It wasn't until the afternoon that I got the chance to talk to Katie in private. I asked her to come to the games room. "Don't bring David," I warned her. "He's hopeless at keeping secrets."

When we got there, she asked at once, "What's the big secret?"

I didn't know how to begin. How could I ask her the thing that was really on my mind – has your mum done something terrible? Is that why she's in hiding?

"Look at this," I said, showing her the card the detective had given me. "The woman who gave me this – the detective – she was here today. In the hotel."

Katie seemed interested rather than alarmed. "Really? Did she arrest anybody?"

"She's not that kind of detective. She was looking for somebody, but not to arrest them. At least I don't think so."

"Who was she looking for?"

"You. And your mum."

"Oh!" Just for a second then, she looked quite scared. "Did you tell her we were here?"

"No."

"Why not?"

"I'm not sure. I think because... well, because your

mum doesn't want anyone to know she's here. Does she?"

She shook her head.

"Is Gray your real name?" I asked, but she didn't answer.

"Look, don't worry. I'm on your side," I told her, wondering if I really was. "I just need to find out what's going on."

"I don't *know* what's going on," she whispered. "Mam never tells me much. Ask me no questions, she says, and I'll tell you no lies."

"So you don't know who she's afraid of?"

She shook her head again.

I said, "But she is afraid of someone. She has nightmares that somebody's coming to get her. You've no idea who it is?"

"No." She swallowed hard. "He nearly got *me* once, though."

"What do you mean?"

"I was playing out after school – this was when we lived in Prestatyn. Everything was normal then, I went to school and everything. This car stopped beside my friend and me. He said, 'You're Katie Martin, aren't you?' and I said yes, and he said to get in the car, he was going to take me to see my dad."

I stared at her. "You didn't get in, did you? Don't you know not to talk to strange men in cars?"

"Look, I was only eight at the time. And I really did want to see my dad. I don't know anything about him. Mam says he went away when I was just a baby."

"So what happened?"

"Josie – that was my friend – shouted at me not to get in the car. Then Mam came running out and grabbed me. The man had hold of my other arm and it felt like they were pulling me apart. Mam screamed at Josie to call the police, and then he let go and drove away."

"Scary," I said. "Who was he?"

"Mam wouldn't tell me. She said he was a bad man, and we would never be safe now he knew where we were; we had to move right away. We only took the things we could carry. I had to leave my hamster and all my toys with Josie... Mam said we'd go back for them, but we never did."

"And ever since then, you've been hiding from this man?"

"Yes."

"What was he like – can you remember?"

"Not really. It all happened so fast. I think he had dark hair and a moustache. And sort of... hungry eyes."

"Did he catch up with you in Blackpool? Was that why you moved?"

"I don't know. Mam thought somebody was keeping watch on the hotel we were in. It wasn't that man, but it could have been somebody working for him, she said."

"Maybe it was nothing to do with you," I said.

"Yeah. But Mam said best to be on the safe side. She always tells me, keep your head down. Stay quiet. Don't get noticed, and if anyone does notice you, move on somewhere else. You can't be too careful, she says."

It was a good thing Sarah didn't read the *Daily Mirror*. If she did, she and Katie would already have vanished in the night; by now they would be in Bournemouth or Brighton or Bognor Regis, under another name.

"I get so fed up of it," said Katie wearily. "As soon as I start to like a place, Mam gets scared again and we have to move on. I never have any friends. If I get any toys or books, I know I'll only have to leave them the next time I move. I hate it!"

"I don't blame you," I said.

Katie began to walk restlessly up and down the room, like a zoo animal pacing the length of a cramped cage. Back and forth, back and forth... Suddenly she said, "I really wish I was like you and David. You've got a proper home. You've lived here for years, you've got friends. I wish I could stay here for ever..."

"Thought you said it was a bit of a dump," I said.

"That was before. I've got used to it now," she said, and grinned. "I've even got used to you and David."

I said, "What will your mum do, if she finds out about the detective coming here?"

"Move on again." Her voice was gloomy.

"Even though she doesn't know why the woman's trying to trace you? I mean, maybe it's about something completely different. Say your granny died and left you thousands of pounds in her will –"

"No. It can't be that."

"How do you know?"

"My granny's dead already."

"Well, somebody else then. Your ancient great-aunt in Australia."

"Haven't got an ancient great-aunt in Australia."

"Or your dad, maybe?"

"Oh!" she said, stopping in mid-stride. "Oh. Do you really think..."

"What?"

"Do you really think my dad might be looking for

me? He might feel sorry he walked out. And he wants to see me again, and he and Mam will get back together and we'll be a proper family... Do you think it might happen?"

I thought this was very unlikely, but I didn't say so because of the longing in her face.

"And then – and then we'll have a house of our own, and everything will be all right... Go on, give the detective a ring. Tell her we're here. I want my dad to find us!"

"Katie, stop! Think for a minute. What if it isn't your dad?"

"But you said..."

"I only said it *could* be. We don't know. It might just as easily be your enemy trying to trace you."

"Oh. Yes..." She went from joy to utter misery. "But how can we find out?"

"I don't know. Give me time, maybe I can think of a way... but don't say a word to your mum. Not yet."

"What's that noise?" she said suddenly.

"Only an ambulance or something." The noise came from out in the street; it got louder and louder. Through the high, barred window we could see the flashing light. Then we heard hurrying feet on the front steps, just above our heads.

Katie said, "What's going on?"

I said, "Probably nothing much. It will be an old lady who's fallen downstairs, or got stuck in the lift." We went to see. David met us on the stairs; he looked frightened.

"It's Sarah. She's quite bad – Mum rang for the ambulance –"

The ambulance people were struggling to get a

stretcher down the steep attic stairs. It didn't look like a comfortable ride, but Sarah's eyes were closed and she never moved.

"Mam!" Katie cried. "What's happened to her?"

My mum put an arm round Katie's shoulder. "It's all right, darling. She's not very well, but they'll soon have her in hospital."

"Is she going to *die*?"

"Of course she's not going to die, sweetheart. She's unconscious, that's all. Let's move out of the way so they can get her into the lift."

"Mam... Mam..." Katie whimpered, and my mother held her close. "Don't you worry, my love. She's going to be all right, you'll see. And we'll look after you – don't you worry, now."

The door of the lift closed slowly and it started to descend. Sarah was gone.

Chapter 11

Serious

Katie spent that night on our sofa – although I don't think she slept very much. In the morning her eyes looked puffy and red, as if she'd spent half the night crying.

What could it be like to know that the one person who cared about you was seriously ill? I couldn't imagine it. If *my* mum was rushed into hospital, I would still have Dad – and David, Granny and Auntie Chris, and all my friends. Katie had absolutely no one.

"We'll look after you," Mum had told her, but we were not her family; we'd only known her for a few weeks. And Mum and Dad were so busy – extra busy, with Sarah out of action. "Keep an eye on Katie for me, won't you?" Mum said to David and me as she hurried off to the dining-room.

After breakfast Mum found time to ring the hospital for news of Sarah.

"Is she all right?" said Katie eagerly. "Can I go and see her?"

"I don't know if she's well enough to be visited just yet," said Mum. "She's got something called meningitis."

"What's that – is it serious?" I asked.

Mum gave me a look which meant: Why can't you keep your big mouth shut?

"It is fairly serious," Mum told Katie. "But we hope they've spotted it in time, and they're giving her all the right medicines. They're doing everything they can."

"Is it catching?" said Dad. "That's all we need. MENINGITIS OUTBREAK IN SEASIDE HOTEL."

Mum gave him another of her looks. "Come on," she said, "get a move on, everybody. Katie, love, could you give us a hand in the bedrooms?"

What a slave-driver, I thought – making Katie work at a time like this. But then, maybe she would rather have something to do to take her mind off the worry.

Sarah was very ill for days. The first time Mum took Katie to the hospital, they were not allowed into her room; they could only look in through a glass panel in the door. Sarah lay asleep, or unconscious, and Katie came home even more white and anxious than before.

"I shouldn't have taken her," Mum said to Dad. "But the hospital said Sarah had improved slightly. If that's true then I hate to think what she was like before."

"Is she going to make it?" Dad asked her.

"God knows. That poor kid..."

After a few days, though, Sarah was much better. Still in bed and very weak, at least she was conscious, able to talk to Katie and hold her hand. Katie began to believe that her mum wasn't going to die after all.

"It will be ages before Sarah's back to work, I'm afraid. We need to get someone temporary, what with Easter coming up," Mum said.

Dad grunted. "I told you it was a mistake taking Sarah on. Now we're doing her work as well as our own, *and* taking Katie to the hospital every day. It would have been better if we'd never seen the pair of them."

"Oh Terry, you wouldn't talk like that if you'd been there this afternoon. Sarah kept thanking me for looking after Katie, and saying how lucky she is to have us. If she'd got ill in her last place, she said, Katie would most likely have ended up in care."

"Best place for her," said Dad. "As I keep reminding you, we're not a charity."

Mum said fiercely, "Don't you try to tell me Katie's not earning her keep. She's helped me every day this week, and she's a good little worker."

"Terrific. Next thing, we'll get prosecuted for using child labour."

"You've been using it for years," I said from the doorway.

"Jake! I thought you were in bed," said Mum, and sighed. "No privacy in this place, is there?"

By now Katie had gone back to sleeping in her own room, but in the daytime she was often in our flat, or hanging about in the games room. She was a pale shadow of her normal lively self. You could see she had a lot on her mind; of course I blamed it on Sarah's illness.

But something else was troubling her, too.

"Jake," she whispered one day, "have you thought about... you know... that phone call?"

"You what?"

"Phoning the detective woman. Oh, you know... about my dad."

"Er... not really. There hasn't been time." What with Sarah being ill and the extra work, not to mention practising for the Fun Run, I had completely forgotten about the detective's visit.

"Because if it is my dad, I really want to know. When Mam was so ill, I got dead scared... I thought I was going to be left all on my own."

I understood. Even a father who'd walked out on her as a baby would be better than no one at all.

"Look, would you mind if I told someone about it? A friend of mine. He might have some ideas." It was Neddy I was thinking of. Neddy would know what to do.

"He won't tell anyone else, will he?" she said anxiously.

"No, of course not."

In the end I told both Neddy and Ben, making them swear to secrecy. (Ben was my best friend, and anyway he knew some of the story already.)

"Interesting," said Neddy. "The mother – do you think she's quite sane?"

"Seeing enemies everywhere, you mean?" I said.

"Yes. Enemies who may not actually exist, except in her own mind. There's a word for that – paranoid."

"Just because she's paranoid," said Ben, "doesn't prove they're not out to get her."

"Katie remembers someone trying to kidnap her," I said. "*That* was real."

Neddy said, "Yes, but the mother's reaction was odd. Why didn't she simply tell the police? There was no need to leave everything and go on the run."

"And then in Blackpool," I said, "Sarah got scared because she thought the hotel was being watched.

Maybe she imagined it, maybe it was police watching out for drug dealers or something. There's no proof it was anything to do with Sarah. She didn't hang around long enough to find out."

"Which was wise, if the enemy is real," said Ben.

"There's also the detective," I said. "She's real all right."

"But perhaps not an enemy. Do you think she would tell us anything about the person she's working for?" asked Neddy.

"No," I said gloomily. "Confidential, she said."

"As I see it, there are two possibilities," Neddy said briskly. "One, it was Katie's father who sent the detective out looking for her. If so – no problem. We fix up a meeting, they hug each other and cry, just like on TV except that Cilla won't be there. But the other possibility..."

"Yes?"

"The other possibility is that the mysterious client is Sarah's enemy. On balance I think that's rather more likely."

"I've tried telling Katie that," I said, "but she doesn't believe me. She really wants to meet this person. She's convinced herself that it's her dad."

"We could still fix up a meeting," said Neddy thoughtfully, "as long as it's somewhere safe, with lots of people around. Where there's no chance he could hurt her or steal her away."

"How about the station?" I suggested. "Or the shopping mall?"

Neddy said, "I was actually thinking of the pier. No traffic, so she couldn't be bundled into a car. He couldn't run off with her – he'd get stopped at the turnstiles."

"What if he simply decides to chuck her into the sea?" said Ben.

"Good point. We'd better make sure we're close by in case of trouble."

"We could be fishing off the edge of the pier," I said.

"Not you, Jake," said Neddy. "The detective woman might come along too, and recognise you."

"So what if she does?"

"If she does, you idiot, she'll make the connection with Sea View. We don't want that. If her client *isn't* Katie's dad, we don't want to give away any information about where she lives."

Ben said, "Are you sure this is safe? Maybe we should tell a grown-up."

"Like who?" I said. "Sarah's ill; Mum and Dad are too busy to want to know. They'll just tell Katie not to be silly. Anyway, what could possibly go wrong?"

Chapter 12

The Fun Run

"Ringing the detective would be too risky," I explained to Katie. "She might be able to trace the phone call, or she could recognise my voice. Or I might give something away by accident – a clue about where we live, I mean."

She looked puzzled.

I said, "If it *isn't* your dad, then we don't want him to know this address, do we? So be very careful when you talk to him, until we know for sure who he is."

"What are we going to do then, if we can't phone her?"

"Write a letter."

"Oh... but that will take ages."

"Better safe than sorry," I said, probably sounding just like her mum.

We worked out what to put in the letter.

If your client wants to meet Katie Martin, tell him to be on the pier on Sunday at 3 pm, opposite the candy-floss stall.

By now it was Thursday. "The letter won't get there in time," Katie objected.

Neddy said, "Not by post, no. But I'm going to

deliver it personally. The Fountain Square Courier Service – swift, efficient and 100 per cent reliable (flat tyres permitting)."

"And even cheaper than the postman," I said.

Ben said, "Joke for the Day. Why do postmen wear blue braces?"

"I don't know," I said, humouring him because he'd been rather quiet lately. "Why do postmen wear blue braces?"

"To keep their trousers up."

"Ha ha."

"Oh, I wish it was Sunday," said Katie. "I can't wait."

"I wish it was Sunday too," said Ben.

"Why?"

"Because by then the Fun Run will be over."

The Fun Run... I was looking forward to it, myself. I knew I could easily do the distance; the weather forecast was reasonable; it would all be a bit of a laugh.

"You worry too much," I said to Ben, as we lined up for the start. "You're twice as fit as some of this lot."

There were about two hundred people taking part – serious runners at the front, kids in silly outfits at the back, Ben and me somewhere in the middle. Darren wormed his way in to join us.

"Can I run with you?" he asked.

Ben said, "Sure. But remember – if you fall and break both legs, don't come running to me."

I said, "I thought you were running with Loz and Macaulay and them."

Darren looked angry. "I *was* going to... but now

they say I can't, there isn't room."

"Isn't room? Well, I suppose Barn does take up most of the width of the road."

"Shhh!"

A ripple of movement went through the crowd of runners, and died into stillness. The polar bear (Mr Wild) raised his noble white head, as if to sniff the air. The two halves of the pantomime horse got their act together, the crazy hat-wearers tightened their strings...

Bang went the starting pistol. We were off!

The first half-mile was along the High Street, which had been cordoned off for us. Spectators waved and smiled; Ben's mum was there, with his sister. (My dad had said he would try to be there for the finish.)

Ben was doing well, not stretching himself, just matching my pace. The runners had begun to string out – over-optimistic sprinters leading the way, but we would overtake them in the end. Not far behind us were the Pump Street crew; I could hear Barn breathing in great blowy gasps, like a horse. What would *he* be like in another mile or two? Next time I looked round, he and his friends had fallen well behind.

Now we turned northwards off the main road, onto the country lane that would take us around the Basin. This road had not been closed to traffic, because it led to a few lonely farms and cottages which couldn't be reached from any other direction. We had been warned to listen out for cars and to keep on the right side of the road.

"How far have we done?" Darren gasped. "Two miles?"

"You're joking. Just coming up for a mile – there'll

be a checkpoint pretty soon."

We moved into the hedge to let a car crawl past. Round a few more corners, and there was the checkpoint, with several eager stewards ready to stamp our cards.

Much to my surprise, the Pump Street crowd arrived close behind us. (There were only three of them, but with Barn present, three's a crowd.) They stopped to have a drink of water and chat up the girl stewards, as if they had all the time in the world. Barn seemed to have got his second wind; his breathing had settled down – you could hardly tell he'd been running.

"Come on," I said to Darren and Ben. Darren was looking far from happy by now.

A few more twists of the road, and hedges gave way to fences, with nothing to shelter us from the cold wind blowing across the Basin. That wind could mean trouble; it was sideways on at the moment, but in another mile or so it would be right in our faces.

Far ahead I could see the flag that marked the next checkpoint. The leading runners – serious marathon contenders from Y12 – had passed it already; they were just visible as small, bright dots strung out along the curve of the Basin. We were still up with the main bunch (somewhere towards the back, because most of them were older than us), but Darren's pace was slowing.

"Why didn't you do a bit of training beforehand?" I said impatiently.

"Didn't think I needed to," he gasped. "You two go on. Don't wait for me."

I would have done, but Ben said, "What's the hurry? You said yourself, Jake, it's not a race."

"Okay. But don't stand still, Darren. We'll walk until you get a bit of breath back."

A white van came up behind us and beeped impatiently. I recognised the driver – Harrison Burton. He must have come to cheer his brother on, I thought. But no; before the next checkpoint the van turned off the road and disappeared into a belt of trees.

By now we were out on our own; the pantomime horse and his friends were a long way behind, the serious runners a long way in front. All at once, I blinked. Between us and the main pack, three runners had appeared as if from nowhere.

"Look at that!" I said. "The Pump Street lot. How did they get there?" There was no mistaking the figure of Barn, even at a distance.

"They didn't pass us, I know they didn't," said Ben. "They must have found a short cut." But even as he said it, he realised it was impossible. There were no short cuts unless you were prepared to swim across the Basin.

Suddenly it clicked. "They *did* pass us," I said. "You just didn't see them."

"Oh, you mean –"

"Yeah. Macaulay's big brother gave them a lift."

"But that's not fair!" Ben cried. "All that training I did... and that lot are driving around in a van!"

I looked at Darren. "You knew about this, didn't you? You were going to be in on it too."

"Yeah. So what?" He booted a stone along the road. "All in a good cause, though, innit? I mean, Barn wouldn't make it beyond Checkpoint One on his own two feet. He wouldn't raise much money for the poor and hungry then. Would he?"

"It's still not fair," Ben muttered. "We should tell someone."

"No!" Darren looked scared. "They'll think it was me that grassed on them. They'll do me in. Ever seen Barn in a bad mood?"

Ben and I exchanged doubtful looks.

"Leave it," I said. "Let's just concentrate on getting round the course. We'll talk about it later."

Chapter 13

Taxi

Just before the checkpoint, the white van overtook us again.

"Going on to make his next pick-up," I said. "Now that should be interesting. Where's he going to stop?"

Beyond Checkpoint 2, the road curved round the north side of the Basin, across acres of desolate, marshy fields. It was as flat and open as a windswept beach. Bad news for us – heading straight into the wind with nothing to shelter us. But equally bad for Barn and his mates.

"I don't see how the van is going to stop for them," said Ben, "not without being seen."

"Maybe he's got a fog machine in the back of the van," I said. "Or a helicopter ready to air-lift them to the next checkpoint."

"Oh yeah, like nobody's going to notice a helicopter," Darren muttered. (Sometimes I think Darren has as much sense of humour as a dead goldfish.) We got our cards stamped at the checkpoint and snatched a quick drink. Darren would have poured about fifteen cups of water down his neck if I hadn't stopped him.

"Can't we leave him behind?" I muttered to Ben.

"Oh, give him a chance. We're nearly half-way round now."

Yes, but the worst was still to come: a long, straight stretch with the wind dead against us. By now the white van was far down the road.

"They must actually intend to *run* to the next checkpoint," said Ben. "Do you think they'll make it?"

"I wouldn't take any bets on it." I was thinking that the same applied to Darren, but he surprised me by breaking into a trot. After about a quarter of a mile we overtook Barn, who looked like someone trying to run up a down escalator – lots of effort but hardly any progress. A little further on, Loz had stopped by the side of the road, coughing dreadfully.

"That's what smoking does to your lungs," I remarked to Darren.

"Don't mention smoking," he gasped. "I'm dying to sit down and have a fag."

The wind blew in gusts as if it wanted to push us back the way we'd come. A few spots of rain stung our faces. So much for the good weather forecast! But we ploughed on, jogging when Darren felt able to, walking when he didn't. The polar bear ambled past, giving us a friendly wave; soon after, the horse's head and front legs approached at a canter.

"What happened to your other half?" I called.

"He had to stop. One of his shoes fell apart."

"And I suppose you couldn't find a blacksmith. What a shame."

Ben said, "Horses have got six legs, did you know? Forelegs at the front and two at the back." The horse didn't seem to think this was funny.

About a hundred metres before Checkpoint 3, Macaulay had stopped to wait for his friends.

"Barn looks in a bad way," I told him. "Maybe you'd better send for a taxi." Macaulay glared at me, but I kept my face quite expressionless.

"What did you go and say that for?" Darren hissed, once we had gone past.

"What are you on about? It was a perfectly innocent remark. I said 'taxi', didn't I? Not 'dirty white van driven by his big brother'."

"Shut up, just shut up." For now we were at the checkpoint.

The stewards here looked absolutely freezing. They were walking about, rubbing their hands, trying to keep warm. Only Neddy looked quite comfortable, but then he was in training – having spent hours sitting still in a cold, damp hide. He had actually brought his binoculars with him to use during quiet spells.

"Seen anything interesting?" I asked him as he stamped my card.

"Not really. Too many people coming and going."

I lowered my voice. "If you want to see something really interesting, then keep an eye on the Pump Street lot after they pass you. I bet you a fiver to a piece of bubble-gum that they don't stay on the proper course. In fact, I know where they'll go... along the track towards those farm buildings." This was an easy guess – it was the only bit of cover in sight.

"Why?" asked Neddy.

"Never you mind. Just observe."

We were off again. The farm I had noticed was set back from the road with a driveway leading to it. As we got closer, I saw that it wasn't a farm any more but somebody's house, or perhaps a holiday home for Piggies. (A working farm always has bits of old machinery lying around; this place was far too tidy.)

And there was the dirty white van, tucked away in the yard between house and stables. You could only see it when you were directly opposite; certainly no one at the checkpoint would know it was there.

What would Barn and his friends say, if anyone asked why they were leaving the proper course? They probably had an excuse ready – such as needing the loo. Once they were inside the van, with its painted rear windows, they would be as good as invisible.

"Got to tie my shoe," I said to the others. "You go on – I'll catch you up." I had some vague idea of waiting at the end of the driveway until the Pump Street mob came along, so that they wouldn't dare to get aboard the van. Yes, I know it was a very foolish move, but I was annoyed.

Something was happening, though. An angry voice came from the direction of the house.

"Would you kindly explain what you're doing here?"

A big man was standing beside the van, holding a large and muddy dog on a lead. He looked as if he had just come back from a long walk and was not expecting visitors. "What are you doing in my driveway?" he bellowed.

"Oh... er... nothing," said Harrison, winding down his window. "That is – it's to do with the Fun Run. You know... for charity."

The man stared at him. "Fun Run or no Fun Run, I'll thank you to get your decrepit vehicle off my property."

This seemed to annoy Harrison. "Oh yeah? If it's your property, why is there a *To Let* sign at the end of the drive?"

Saltmarsh House, the sign read. *To Let, short or long term, ring 866813.*

"If I am paying the rent, then it's my property," said the man angrily. "So kindly remove yourself. Do you want me to complain to the organisers of this ludicrous Fun Run? Or would you prefer to have me turn my dog loose on you?"

The dog growled menacingly. It was big, all right. It looked as if it could quite easily take a leap through Harrison's window and have him by the throat.

"Okay, okay," said Harrison. "No need to get your knickers in a twist. I'm going." He revved up his engine; a great cloud came out of the exhaust as he shot down the drive.

I had tied my shoelace about fifteen times over, but I did it once more just to see the expressions of Barn and friends as they left the checkpoint. First of all puzzlement (why was Harrison coming out into plain view?), then anger (why was he driving off into the distance?) then finally despair, like people who have missed the last bus on a pouring wet Saturday night. I did not think the van would find another hiding place until almost at the next checkpoint. Would any of them make it?

The man from Saltmarsh House drove out in a grey Volvo. By the look of his face, he was still fuming. I moved on hurriedly, in case he started yelling at me for standing in *his* entrance, breathing *his* air. (Typical Piggy – rent a place for a week or two and they start thinking they own it.) Out in the road, he put his foot down; he was going much too fast for the country lane. With any luck he would crash into the bridge not far ahead.

I put my foot down too, wondering where Ben and Darren had got to. The road swept around in a wide curve; now I could see the hump-backed bridge that took it over the river, not far from the edge of the Basin. The Volvo had already crossed the bridge and was speeding away. But where was Ben?

I crossed the bridge – and there he was, sitting by the roadside with one leg stretched out in front of him. His face was twisted with pain. Darren knelt beside him, looking worried.

"See? I knew it," said Ben, attempting to smile. "I knew I'd never get all the way round."

Chapter 14

All in a good cause

"What happened?"

"Some stupid idiot nearly ran us down," said Darren. "He came over the bridge much too fast, right in the middle of the road."

"Did he actually hit you?"

"Would have, but we jumped clear. I'm okay – grazed my leg, that's all. But Ben landed funny."

"I think I've done my knee in," said Ben.

Darren said, "The idiot! He must have seen what happened, but he never even slowed down. Wish I'd got his number."

"I know where he lives," I said. "But never mind that now. Can you move your leg, Ben?"

"Every time I try, it really hurts."

I looked down at it helplessly, wishing I could remember anything useful about First Aid. Keep the patient still – no, that was for neck injuries. Put him in the recovery position – no, not if he was still conscious.

Looking around, I tried to decide which was the nearest checkpoint. Three and Four were both about half a mile away; I thought Four was slightly closer.

But would there be anyone there who knew what to do?

There was supposed to be a First Aid car driving around the course. It had gone past while we were at Checkpoint Three – it might not come round again for ages.

"I'll run on to Checkpoint Four and get help," I said.

"No! Stay here, Jake," said Ben pleadingly. "Can't someone else go?"

Darren would willingly have done it, but just then three girls from Y10 came over the bridge. They promised to send someone back from Checkpoint Four. Just in case they forgot, we told the next group too, and the next. The Fun section of the Fun Run was still trailing past in tattered costumes and wind-blown hats; most of them were walking now, not running.

Ben began to look restless. "My leg feels a bit better," he said. "Maybe I could walk on further."

"Don't be daft," I said. "Why?"

"For the money, of course. I've only done three checkpoints instead of five – I'll only get about half the sponsor money."

"Who cares about that?" Starving people in Africa seemed a long way away just then.

But Ben said obstinately, "I want to give it a try. Can you and Darren lift me up?"

With the help of two passing Hawaiian Islanders, we managed to heave him up onto his good leg. But when he tried to put his other foot on the ground, he cried out in pain.

"Sit him down again," I said.

"No!" he said through clenched teeth. "I *can* walk, if I can hold onto you and Darren." He put an arm round each of our shoulders, and using us like a pair of crutches he managed to hobble slowly forwards. He was sweating; I could only guess how much pain he was in.

"This is stupid," said Darren. "It's not worth half-killing yourself for. What difference will it make?"

Ben muttered something I couldn't quite hear.

"You what?"

"I said, eighty quids' worth of difference. Could be several people's lives."

"Yeah, and all for the sake of people you've never even seen," I said. "What's the point? You won't get any thanks for it."

We stopped for a rest, leaning Ben against a gate-post. He was beginning to shiver, which was not surprising. We were all wearing running gear, thin vests and shorts; the wind seemed to blow right through us and out the other side.

"I've had an idea," I said. "If you're determined to finish the race... I could be you and you could be me."

"What do you mean?"

"Like this. We swop our race cards. Then you sit here and wait to be rescued. I've hardly got any sponsors – it won't make much odds whether my card says three miles or five. I'll finish the run, and your card will get stamped, and you can collect the money. Pass GO and collect £200."

But I already knew he wouldn't agree.

"Why not?" said Darren. "I would. It's all in a good cause."

"You're wasting your breath," I told Darren. "Don't you know Ben never does anything wrong? God wouldn't like it, see. God watches Ben all the time."

"Oh, does he? Pity he wasn't looking out for us when that car went past," said Darren.

"He was," Ben murmured, so quietly that I almost didn't hear.

We were all getting tired. Why didn't anyone come to help us? We stopped for another rest, and this time it was harder to get going again. Three white mice overtook us, followed by Fred and Wilma Flintstone, the back end of the horse, and even – oh, the shame of it – Loz, Barn and Macaulay.

They looked at us curiously. "This your good deed for the year, then, Darren?" said Loz.

"Shut up."

"I hope he's going to make it worth your while," said Macaulay. "How much are you sponsored for, kid?"

"Forty quid a mile," Ben managed to say.

"Forty quid – not bad. Not bad at all for a cripple. How much is he giving you, Darren – ten per cent?"

"Now me," said Barn, "guess how much I'm getting a mile. Go on, have a guess. You won't believe it but I'm getting sixty –"

"Sixty pence a mile," Loz cut in swiftly. "Why does he do it, eh? You may well ask, when all he's going to raise is, er..."

"Three quid," said Macaulay. He shot Barn a look of warning.

"Enough of this idle chit-chat," said Loz. "Enjoy yourselves, kids. Happy Fun Running!"

Now what was all that about? But there was no time to wonder, because a steward came hurrying to meet us. "The First Aid car's on its way," she said. "We rang them on our mobile phone. Why don't you sit down and wait?"

"No," said Ben grimly. "I've got to get to the checkpoint."

We could see it by now, about four hundred metres away, and he stepped out bravely. It was the longest four hundred metres I've ever travelled. His weight on my shoulder grew heavier and heavier; Darren and I were almost carrying him by the end. We made it, though, and he saw his card being stamped.

"If you think we're taking you on to the next checkpoint, you can think again," I said.

The First Aid car arrived, and we laid him down thankfully on the back seat. It carried him off to hospital for an X-ray. He was too exhausted even to wave goodbye.

He had only completed four miles instead of five, but I reckoned most people would pay the full amount once they knew what he'd done.

"Wasn't he brave?" said the steward.

"Either that or stupid," said Darren. "Come on, let's finish this."

We set off on the last mile, feeling light and free with no extra weight to carry.

"Know something?" said Darren. "I was going to keep some of my sponsor money, but I won't now. I'm going to hand in all of it."

"Keep it?" I said. "But you couldn't. The school will check the money you hand in against your sponsor form."

"Yeah, sure. But say you had two sponsor forms and you only handed in one? The school would never know about half your sponsors."

"Aha... so *that's* why the Pump Street lot were so

keen to help the poor and needy. I thought at the time it was strange," I said. "Sixty quid a mile, old Barn was about to say, wasn't he? I wonder how much of it will go straight into his own pocket."

"Most of it, you bet," said Darren. "Poor and needy – he thinks that means him."

"Something must be done about this," I said.

"If you say so. Just don't mention my name, okay?"

Chapter 15

On the pier

It turned out that Ben hadn't broken anything. He had damaged a ligament, whatever that meant.

"A ligament is... well, I think it sort of joins your bones and muscles together," said Ben. His leg was wrapped in a long tube-shaped bandage; he was supposed to rest it as much as possible and walk with a crutch. "If I'm careful, the doctor said it should mend okay."

"I still think we should report that driver to the police," I said.

Ben looked worried. "Are you sure it was the guy from Saltmarsh House? I mean, you didn't *see* him do it, and we didn't notice much about the car that nearly hit us. It was grey, that's all I remember."

"Yes," I said, "but how many grey cars were speeding on that road yesterday afternoon? There wasn't much traffic at all. That's why I noticed Harrison's van... hey, was it definitely a car that passed you, not a van?"

"I think so but I couldn't swear to it."

In the end we left it. I was still convinced that the man from Saltmarsh House had been the one. But he was just a Piggy; he would be gone in a week or two, anyway. And as Ben said, it wasn't like he'd actually killed someone. No lasting harm had been done.

"Heard about the man who broke his arm?" said Ben. "He asked the doctor, 'Will I be able to play the cello when my arm gets better?' 'Of course you will,' the doctor told him. 'That's good,' he said, 'because I couldn't play it before.'"

"There is one problem," said Neddy, whacking Ben on his good leg to shut him up. "Ben won't be able to go with Katie to the pier this afternoon."

"I could go instead," I said eagerly. I wanted to see the Mysterious Client for myself.

Neddy said, "Yes, I think you'll have to. We might need you in case there's trouble. But try to disguise yourself a bit, won't you? Just in case the detective turns up, and recognises you."

"What d'you mean, disguise myself? You want me to go as a polar bear or the back half of a horse?"

"No, just a Piggy. You know – sunglasses, baseball cap, *I love Westhaven* T-shirt. That ought to pass unnoticed on the pier, all right. Oh, and bring a crab-line."

At half past two (far too early, but Katie insisted), we set out for the pier. Katie was wearing what looked like her best dress and some of Mum's lipstick. I hadn't been able to borrow a Westhaven T-shirt – and I certainly wasn't going to buy one – but I did have a plastic bucket and spade borrowed from Ben's little sister.

It was ages since I'd been on the pier, because you have to pay to go on, and what are you actually getting? Not a lot. A kiddies' funfair, a cafe, a few stalls, and a cold, breezy walk to the end of the pier and back. Quite a few Piggies were out there, though you couldn't describe the weather as warm. Yesterday's wind was still gusting around, snapping the flags like whips, and making white-caps far out on the cold grey-green sea.

Before ten to three we were all in place: Katie on a bench opposite the candy-floss stall, Neddy and myself at the edge of the pier about ten metres away. We had the crab-line out in case anyone wondered why we were there, but we didn't bother to inspect it. (Only Piggies ever go crabbing off the pier – the crabs take the bait all right, but the pier is so high, you can't haul them in before they let go again.)

"Remember, Katie," Neddy had said, "you don't know us. Don't talk to us, don't even look at us. But if there's any... how shall I put it... any trouble, then just shout, and we'll be there instantly."

Katie, I could tell, thought we were being stupid. Her dad was coming to see her – how could there be any trouble?

Five to three, and she was eagerly scanning the faces of everyone who walked along the pier. Mostly they were couples or families. I watched her out of the corner of my eye, wondering how she'd react if no one turned up... or even worse, if the wrong person turned up.

The wind brought us the sound of the town centre clock chiming three. No one came up to her; no one, as far as we could see, was watching from a distance; no one paid her any attention.

"Better give it a bit longer," I muttered to Neddy. "He might be late."

Neddy said, "It's possible he's inside the café or somewhere, just watching her."

"Why would he do that?"

"He might be afraid it's a trap."

"Why on earth should he think that?"

"Well, of course he wouldn't think that... unless he meant to do her harm," said Neddy.

I did not much like the matter-of-fact way he said it. "This is all a sort of game to you, isn't it?" I said.

"No, I wouldn't call it a game. More of a mystery – an intriguing mystery. I'd like to get to the bottom of it."

"And you don't care who gets hurt on the way?"

"What *are* you talking about? That's what we're here for, to make sure Katie doesn't get hurt."

"I don't mean *hurt* hurt. I mean let down, disappointed." Heartbroken, is what I really meant, but Neddy would think that was stupid. (Mind you, Neddy of all people ought to understand – he hadn't seen his own father since he was six.)

"Shhh!" he said. "Someone's talking to her."

I glanced ever so casually over my shoulder. It was a mum with two small children. Surely that couldn't be the Mysterious Client?

"I'm all *right*," I heard Katie say crossly. "I'm waiting for my dad."

The woman went away, looking back at her once or twice, as if she could somehow tell that Katie was not all right – far from it.

The long minutes passed. I was so bored that I even hauled in the crab-line, squealing "I've got one! Oh no, it got away!" like a genuine Piggy. At last the town hall clock struck half past three, and Neddy said, "I can't stay around much longer. Grandmother said I absolutely must be back by four because her sister's coming to tea. Great-aunt Lizzie. She's even worse than Grandmother," he said despondently.

Did I mention that Neddy lives with his grandmother, who used to be a headmistress? She is fearsome. I bet she didn't have discipline problems in her school. If Grandmother said be home at four, then Neddy would be home at four.

At twenty to four we coiled up the crab-line and went over to where Katie was sitting.

"Katie, it's time we went home," I said as gently as I could. "We've been here nearly an hour – he won't come now, you know he won't."

"Just ten more minutes," she pleaded. "Maybe his car broke down... ten more minutes. Please!"

Neddy looked at his watch. "I really must go," he said, "but you don't need me, anyway. He's not going to show up."

"Okay – go then," I said. "We'll give it another ten minutes."

"Just be careful as you're leaving." He lowered his voice. "Make sure there's nobody following you."

"Don't talk daft. What was that word of yours – paranoid?"

All the same, when (more than half an hour later) Katie finally agreed to leave, I made sure the nearest Piggies were a long way down the pier. I checked that no one suddenly emerged from the cafe or the fun-fair. I kept looking over my shoulder until we were safely outside the turnstiles of the pier.

Walking home, I tried to think of things that might cheer Katie up, but somehow nothing came to mind. She stared into the far distance, just like Queen

Victoria's statue on the promenade; her face seemed carved in stone.

Oh well, at least she wasn't in floods of tears – I don't know how I would have coped with that. We went home in total silence.

Chapter 16

Three-two

That evening, Neddy and I went to see Ben to fill him in on what had happened. He was annoyed that we hadn't come sooner. Trapped at home, with his leg propped up on the bed, he was feeling bored and fed up.

"I would have come as soon as we got back," I said, "but Dad nabbed me to help serve up the Kiddies' High Tea. Lovely, that was. Ten little Piggies, all arguing with each other and smearing ketchup all over everything. One of them put ketchup on his ice-cream."

"At the opposite extreme," said Neddy, "I had tea with Grandmother and Great-aunt Lizzie. Tiny little cucumber sandwiches. Grandmother watching me like a hawk, in case my manners showed her up in front of her sister... I got out as soon as I could."

I said, "Anyway, there's nothing to tell. Nobody turned up."

"Oh... Is Katie upset?"

"Upset? Whatever gives you that idea? Sang and danced all the way home."

Neddy was looking depressed. "This means we've

come to a dead end. We've no way of finding out anything more."

"Tough," I said. "Sherlock Fields, the great detective, will have to find some other mystery to solve. How about the Case of the Missing Sponsor Money?"

I told Neddy my suspicions about the Pump Street fun-runners. "And Darren was going to do the same thing – until you changed his mind, Ben."

"Me? How? I never said a thing."

"It wasn't what you said, it was what you did. We couldn't decide whether you were a hero or an idiot –"

"Both," said Neddy. "In fact most heroes are idiots."

"But anyway, Darren decided to be a good little boy and hand in all his sponsor money. Mind you, that was yesterday. He may have changed his mind again by now."

Neddy said, "As for Loz and Barn and Macaulay, they weren't affected by Ben's shining example. I wonder how we could make them see the error of their ways?"

"Never mind the error of their ways," I said. "We just want to make them hand over the money. Hundreds of pounds, we're talking about here."

"Perhaps another anonymous letter?" Neddy suggested. *"If you do not hand in ALL your sponsor money, the Head will hear about the white van. I have photographic evidence. Yours sincerely, A Fun Run Steward."*

"But we don't have photographic evidence," Ben objected.

"A minor detail," said Neddy. "They don't know that, and we've got to have something to threaten them with."

Ben still looked unhappy. "Your conscience bothering you again?" I said. "Look, that lot are planning to cheat famine victims out of hundreds of pounds. What's one little fib if we can manage to stop them?"

Neddy sighed. "Ben, I wish you'd grow out of these... these ridiculous childish fears. What do you think will happen if you do break the rules once in a while? A giant finger will point at you out of the sky – a huge foot will stamp on you?"

"That's not what I think," said Ben. "You know it isn't."

"Really? But you do believe that God's got his eye on you all the time, right?" said Neddy. He was enjoying this. He liked an argument, especially one he was sure he could win.

"Not like *that*," Ben said. "Not like your grandmother, always ready to criticise and punish you. God isn't like that at all. He watches over us because... well, he cares about us. Same as my mum watching me do the Fun Run – because she's my mum and she wants me to do well."

Neddy's face had taken on a blank look, which meant he was thinking hard. He said nothing.

Ben went on, "But even if I didn't do too well – if I fell flat on my face right in front of her – Mum wouldn't get mad at me. She would help me get up and start again. And that's exactly like what God does, too, if we do something wrong –"

"Wait a minute," Neddy interrupted. "That's what you *imagine* God being like. Your ideas about God are based on your own parents. When I try to imagine God, he turns out like my grandmother – stern and critical and always making rules. What about you, Jake? What do you see if you try to imagine God?"

"I dunno. An old man with a long white beard, up in the sky somewhere."

Neddy said, "In other words, someone at a distance, too busy to notice you much?"

I nodded.

"Rather like your own parents, in fact?" He turned back to Ben. "So who's right? We all imagine something different. What makes you think your version is right and mine's wrong?"

Neddy sounded angry now, for some reason, but Ben answered quite calmly.

"Alan was talking about this at Friday Club. He said there are two ways you can find out what God's really like. One, by getting to know him yourself..."

"*Imagining* you know him, you mean," said Neddy.

"And two, by what Jesus said about him. It's all written down in the Bible. He said God's like a father – a good father, one who loves his children and listens to them and knows all about them –"

"Yes, I do know what a father is traditionally meant to be like," said Neddy coldly. "There's no need to go on and on. But why should what Jesus said have any relevance to me? Why should he know what God was like, any better than I do?"

"Because he was God's son," said Ben.

"Who says?"

"Well – he did. He said he was God's son."

"So? Mad people in mental hospitals say the same thing. They say they're God, or Napoleon, or Hitler, or a jam sandwich. Just because he said it, doesn't prove it's true."

Two-one to Neddy, I thought. But Ben came back strongly.

"What about all the miracles Jesus did? You know – making people better. Calming down a storm. Bringing dead people back to life. He didn't do those things for fun – he did them so that people would know who he really was."

"Two-all," I said, but nobody was listening.

"There's no scientific proof -" Neddy began.

"Scientific? That's a good word," said Ben. "Scientists are supposed to be open-minded, aren't they? Until they get proof one way or the other. But you've already decided Christians have got it wrong. Not because of evidence... just because you don't *want* to believe it. Is that scientific?"

Three-two! Amazing! Even more amazing, Neddy didn't have an immediate answer.

"Ding-ding! End of round two," I said. "And Neddy, the previously undefeated champion, slinks back to his corner, while Ben, who went into this fight with odds of ten to one against -"

"Shut up, Jake," said Neddy savagely. "Look, I've got to go. I've got homework to finish."

I left too; it was six o'clock and getting dark. As we crossed the Square, I happened to notice a small blue car with a man in it, reading the paper. Reading the paper? It must be hard to make out even the headlines in the gathering dusk.

"Neddy, come in for a minute," I said, and he followed me into the hotel. "Did you notice a man in a blue car? Reading the paper, or pretending to?"

He shook his head. "What about it? Oh... you mean he might be watching the place?"

Cautiously we looked out of the dining-room window. But there was just an empty space where the blue car had been.

"He's gone. I must be getting over-anxious, like Sarah."

"Well, it's best to be careful," said Neddy. "Are you absolutely positive you weren't followed back here this afternoon?"

"I did check. I'm dead sure nobody followed us off the pier."

"And afterwards?" said Neddy.

"What d'you mean, afterwards?"

"After you left the pier, you idiot. Are you sure you weren't followed then?"

I stared at him. "I don't know. I thought we were safe once we got onto the sea front..."

"You mean you didn't even bother to check? Oh, Jake! Use your brain! There's only one exit from the pier, isn't there?"

"So what?"

"So anyone who knew Katie was on the pier, only had to wait on the sea front until she came out through the turnstile... and then follow her home. Didn't you think of that?"

"No. I suppose I was worried about Katie..."

Neddy said, "Oh, great. So worried about her, you led her enemy straight back here."

"We don't know that," I said. "Maybe no one followed us. Maybe that guy in the car was nothing to do with Katie."

"Talking of Katie," he said, "where is she right now? Do we know?"

"Er... no."

"Well hadn't we better find out?"

I don't think I've ever got up the attic stairs as fast as I did then. David was in the living-room, watching TV.

"Where's Katie?" I shouted.

"Dunno. Haven't seen her all afternoon. Is something wrong?"

"I hope not. She wouldn't go out on her own, would she?"

"Try the games room," said David.

Neddy and I charged down the five flights of stairs to the basement. The games room was empty, apart from two Piglets fighting over a snooker cue. Katie's blue jacket lay abandoned on the window-sill; but of Katie herself there was no sign at all.

Chapter 17

The truth

"What's the matter?" asked Henry. He came out of the wine cellar as we stood in the passage, wondering what on earth to do now. "Seen a ghost, have you?"

"It's Katie," I said. "She's gone..."

"Gone, has she? Now if it was that mother of hers I'd say good riddance. What d'you mean, gone?"

We gabbled out the story.

"What do we do, Henry? Call the police?"

"Now hold on a minute. Have you checked everywhere? Her bedroom? Upstairs, helping your mum?"

I ran upstairs. Dad was in the office, Mum was in the dining-room; no Katie. Up to the attic again – I thumped on Katie's bedroom door. There was no answer, so I tried the door. It seemed to be locked.

"Katie? Are you in there?"

I thought I heard a small sound, so I shouted again. "Katie! I need to know if you're all right..."

"Go away," came a muffled voice. "Just leave me alone."

I obeyed. At least she was safe there, locked in her room right at the top of the building. I found Henry and Neddy in the kitchen. Henry was putting the finishing touches to a trifle; the first diners would soon be arriving, and work must go on.

"It's okay," I said. "She's locked herself in her room. She's upset about this afternoon – you know, her dad not showing up."

"Henry has an interesting theory," said Neddy. "He thinks the enemy and Katie's dad are one and the same person."

"What?"

"Suppose Katie's mum and dad split up," said Henry. "Her mum hates her dad so much that she doesn't want to see him ever again, or for Katie to see him either. So she disappears, taking Katie with her, and tells her all this rigmarole about somebody wanting to kill her. It isn't true – it's just to put the fear of death into Katie, in case her dad tries to get her back. Makes sense, doesn't it?"

"But then, why didn't he come to meet her this afternoon?" I asked.

"He doesn't want to show his hand too soon," said Henry. "He's planning to rescue her from that mother of hers, who is barking mad if you ask me, and give her a decent life and a proper home. In my opinion we should be helping him find her, not hiding her away."

"Hiding who away?" said Mum, coming in from the dining-room.

"Tell your mother. Go on," said Henry. "It's time she knew what that Sarah's been up to." He began to slice up a cucumber at ferocious speed.

As Mum listened to our story, her face grew more and more serious. "This is dreadful," she said. "Why didn't you tell me before?"

"Dreadful is the word," said Henry. "I wouldn't be

at all surprised if that Sarah woman kidnapped Katie when she was a baby. She's not her mother at all. How could she be? They're nothing like each other."

"Henry," said Mum, "if you could just be quiet for one minute, I'll tell you the real reason Sarah's in hiding. She told me all about it in the hospital. I promised I wouldn't tell anyone else unless I absolutely had to, but I really think..."

"Go on, Mum," I said.

"Years ago," said Mum, "when Sarah was only about eighteen, she started going out with a man called Paul. She was very fond of him. When she found out he was already married to somebody else, it came as a shock. But he told her he was going to divorce his wife because they were always arguing – and then he and Sarah would get married.

"Anyway, one night very late he came to see Sarah. He told her his wife had killed herself by driving her car off the edge of a cliff. He was worried that the police would think he had something to do with it – that he'd murdered his wife. So he wanted Sarah to tell the police he couldn't have done it because he'd been at Sarah's flat all evening."

"Give him an alibi, you mean," said Neddy. "Did she agree to do it?"

"Yes. She was in love with the man – she trusted him. When the police questioned her, she told lies and said Paul had been with her the evening his wife died. But the police didn't believe her. They thought Paul's wife had been murdered; they thought she was already dead when the car was sent over the cliff edge. And the only person who wanted her dead was Paul.

"When he was put on trial, Sarah realised that she

would have to tell lies again in court, and by now she was wondering what the truth really was. The man she was in love with – was he really a murderer? If she said what Paul wanted her to say, would she be helping a killer to escape?"

"Whatever did she do?" I asked.

"What she should have done right from the start. She told the truth. And then it all came out, how Paul had asked her to lie about where he was that night. He was found guilty of murdering his wife and went to prison for years and years.

"He was very angry. He had killed his wife for the sake of Sarah, but she had turned against him – that was how he saw it. He wrote to her, telling her he would have his revenge, even if it took him the rest of his life. But at first she didn't worry too much. She met someone else and got married and had Katie..."

"The marriage didn't work out?" said Neddy.

"No. Katie's dad went off and left them when she was only a few months old. But Sarah and Katie managed all right on their own, and Sarah would have forgotten all about Paul, except that every few months a letter would arrive. It would say something like, *I haven't forgotten. I'll get you in the end.*"

"Scary," I said. "Did she tell the police?"

"Yes, and when Paul was due to come out of prison, they helped her move to a new town where she and Katie lived under a different name. She felt safe there for a while –"

"Until he managed to track them down," I said. "Katie told me about it. He tried to kidnap her."

Mum said, "After that, Sarah felt she couldn't trust anyone, not even the police. The only thing she could do was keep moving, keep changing her name... She isn't really called Sarah; her name's Jane Martin. But I can't get used to that."

Henry said, "Of course this could all be a pack of lies. Whatever she calls herself, I wouldn't trust her as far as I could throw her."

"Henry!" Mum was angry now. "You ought to have some sympathy for that poor woman, after all she's been through. I know you've never liked her –"

Neddy interrupted her. "Does Katie know about any of this?"

Mum shook her head. "And Sarah doesn't want her to. She doesn't want Katie to get frightened."

"But how are we going to make sure Katie's safe?" I said. "She must never go outside – not on her own. Not when that man could be waiting to catch her."

"Leave it to me," said Mum. "I'll have a chat with her."

Nothing happened for several days. Sarah was still in hospital ("Best place she could be, really," said Neddy.) Apart from going to visit her with Mum, Katie was not supposed to leave the hotel. She hung around indoors, looking bored and miserable.

Thursday was the first day of the Easter holidays – no holiday for us, though. We were fully booked, we still had no replacement for Sarah, and worst of all it was Henry's day off. In the kitchen, Dad was making even more than his usual mess. A coach had arrived to pick up twenty people who were still waiting for their breakfast. At that moment, a Public Health and Safety man arrived to inspect our fire exits.

"Jake!" Mum called. "Show this gentleman around,

will you, please. As you can see," she said to the safety inspector, "you've picked a bad moment. We're absolutely rushed off our feet. If you'd phoned first..."

"Oh, but we can't give people warning," he said. "The whole idea of a check-up is to take people by surprise, don't you see?"

We didn't argue. Dad says, always be polite to those people, however annoying. If we annoy them, they have the power to make life very difficult for us – even to close us down.

I vaguely recognised this man; perhaps he'd inspected us before. "Where would you like to look first?" I asked him.

"Let's start at the bottom, shall we?"

We went down to the basement. He checked the fire exit in the games room, where Katie was playing darts against herself, and winning. (She was nearly as good at darts as at snooker.) The fire door opened all right, but he grumbled about the dustbins in the yard outside, partly blocking the steps up to the street. I heaved them to one side, which seemed to satisfy him.

"Much better. *Much* better," he said as we went back inside. "Now then, I need to see a copy of your evacuation plan."

I looked at him blankly.

"Evacuation," he said, "in case of fire. You must have a plan of the hotel, with fire assembly points marked on it. It's a legal requirement."

"Oh... I'll have to ask Mum. Won't be a minute."

But it took more than a minute for Mum to find the plans he wanted. I hurried downstairs with them – where was the inspector?

"Katie, have you seen that guy..."

My voice trailed off, because Katie wasn't there. The games room was quite empty. A cold wind blew in through the open fire door.

This time it was no false alarm – this time it was for real. She had vanished.

Chapter 18

Bird-watching

When the police had been and gone, Neddy and I went over to Ben's house. It was quieter there; there were no Piggies demanding to know what was going on, or asking how much longer they would have to wait before they could check out.

All of us, including Ben (who had seen what happened from his window) had told the police everything we knew. Now there was nothing we could do except wait. A trace had been put on our phone in case the kidnapper tried to get in touch. A search was on for the car Ben had seen, which was small and blue, a Fiat possibly – number unknown.

"I might have got the number if that dirty great coach hadn't been in the way," said Ben. "But it all happened so fast. Even if I could walk, I wouldn't have been able to do anything."

"Tell us again what you saw," said Neddy.

"This man came up the steps from the hotel basement. I thought it was a bit odd because nobody except the dustmen ever comes out that way. He was tall and dark-haired and wearing a suit. At first I thought he was carrying a sack over his shoulder – then I saw her fair hair as he laid her down on the seat of the car."

"She wasn't fighting or struggling?" I asked. "Oh. You don't think...?"

"He wouldn't *kill* her," said Neddy. "She's more useful to him alive. Maybe he gave her chloroform or something, just enough to send her unconscious."

I said, "What do you mean, she's more useful to him alive?"

"Think about it," Neddy said. "This guy hates Sarah, not Katie. He's going to use her to get to her mother. You know the kind of thing – meet me on the cliff-top at midnight if you ever want to see your daughter alive again."

I shivered. So much hatred, years and years of it, becoming an obsession, taking over a life – more than one life. Not only Paul's but Sarah's, too.

"He seemed so ordinary," I said. "I thought he was from the Council. I even thought I knew him."

"Knew him?" said Ben. "You'd seen him before?"

Neddy said, "You had, of course. The man in the blue car, remember? Last Sunday evening."

"No," I said. "I hardly saw the man in the car. He was behind a newspaper, and it was nearly dark. If I did see him before, it must have been somewhere else."

I thought and thought, but I couldn't remember. Maybe I'd imagined it.

I had already told the police all I could about the man, but really my description was no better than Ben's – tall, dark-haired, wearing a suit. He was Dad's age or older, and his voice was quite posh. (Was it the voice I recognised, rather than the face? Yes; I was quite sure I'd heard the voice before somewhere. And not too long ago, either.)

"Tell the police," Ben urged me.

"Tell them what? That I've seen or heard him before but I don't know where? Not exactly helpful, is it? Look, I meet dozens of people every week in the hotel. Probably he looked like one of them... And that reminds me, it's time I went. I've got eight bedrooms to do over before two o'clock." Because whatever happened, the work had to go on.

Mum had gone to the hospital, to be with Sarah when the police broke the news to her. I tried not to think about Sarah and what she must be going through. I tried not to think about Katie. Half of this mess was my fault; why hadn't I just minded my own business?

Angrily I scrubbed out baths and ripped sheets off the beds. As I finished Room Nine, I glanced out of the window. Across the Square I noticed a big red "C" on Ben's window-sill. *Come over at once, top priority!* Neddy had seen it too; he was hurrying across the Square. I followed him.

"Well? What is it then?" I demanded. "I hope it's important. Some of us have got work to do."

Ben looked rather embarrassed. "I'm not sure it is important. Maybe it's nothing..."

"Get on with it," I said.

"Well... I was praying about all this. I know you think praying is a load of rubbish, but –"

"Oh get *on* with it."

Ben said, "A sort of picture came into my mind. I saw a bridge. It was that bridge where I nearly got knocked over – you know?"

"Oh. Is that supposed to tell us something?" said Neddy.

"I don't know," said Ben, looking as if he wished he hadn't mentioned it.

Neddy said, "If it's a message from God, I wish he'd speak up a bit. A bridge? Could mean anything. Katie's fallen in the river. Or she's gone on a fun run. Or she's already crossed the bridge to the Great Mansion in the Sky."

"Shut up!" I said, for something had set my memory to work. The bridge... the Fun Run... the man in the grey car...

"It's him. It's him! The man from Saltmarsh House. You know, the one who shouted at Macaulay's brother? That's who he reminded me of."

Neddy stared at me. "Reminded you – okay. But are they the same person?"

"I'm not sure. The voices were alike. But the man at Saltmarsh House had longer hair." I tried to imagine what he would look like with a haircut, and failed. I had only seen him from a distance, for a few short minutes. "And then what about the car? It was a grey Volvo at Saltmarsh House, not a blue Fiat."

Neddy said, "Cars can be changed almost as easily as haircuts. It might have been a hired car or even a stolen vehicle. And Saltmarsh House would be an excellent place to hide somebody... there isn't another house within a mile of it."

"Tell the police," said Ben once more.

"Don't be daft. I'll look a real idiot if they go charging out there and arrest some innocent guy in a grey Volvo."

"But suppose it's really him?"

I said, "If I could just have one more look at him – the man at Saltmarsh House – I'm sure I would know."

"Too dangerous," said Ben. "What if *he* saw *you*?"

Neddy had gone all quiet again. Suddenly he said, "How about a spot of bird-watching? There are several hides round the edge of the Basin; I'm pretty sure there's one near Saltmarsh House..."

"Neddy," I said, "you're a genius."

We hid our bikes behind a water-trough in a field half a mile from Saltmarsh House. Then we walked down to the edge of the Basin and onto the squelching mud. Keeping beyond the reed-beds, we walked along below the high-water mark. Luckily the tide was out.

Now and then I lifted my borrowed binoculars and pretended to scan the horizon. Was that a golden eagle, or maybe an emu?

"It's a seagull," said Neddy with scorn.

"That's what I said. A golden seagull."

It was cold and windy; I was glad when we reached the shelter of the hide. (Or partial shelter, for the wind found its way through every gap in the wooden walls.) Neddy opened a shutter on one of the long narrow windows.

"Look, there's the house," he said.

"Oh great." All I could see was the roof. The tall reeds screened off any view of doors or windows.

"We're not going to see him from here," I said, "unless he decides his chimney needs mending."

Neddy looked crestfallen. "We could go a bit closer, I suppose. But stay behind the reeds."

I crept closer until only a thin layer of reeds stood between me and an open field. Beyond the field was the road, and then the driveway leading to Saltmarsh House. It was still a good distance away; I would need those binoculars. If, that is, anyone ever came out.

There were no signs of life at the house; no lights in any windows, although the weather was dark and gloomy; no cars, whether grey or blue. No noises, either, except the occasional howling of a dog – the loneliest sound in all the world.

"He must have gone out," I whispered. "We could go and have a closer look."

"Risky," said Neddy. "What if he comes back?"

"We'll hear his car, won't we? There's never much traffic on this road. If we hear anything, we'll nip round the back of the farm buildings."

"Okay. But I don't quite see what you're hoping to prove by snooping around his house when he's not there."

We ran across the field, over the road and into the driveway, where for some reason we both slowed down. It was the house, I think, that made me feel nervous, with its six dark staring windows. Was it really empty?

The yard beside the house was definitely empty – apart from the dog. It was tied up on a long chain. When we came near, it stood up and began to growl deep in its throat. It was just as big and mean as I remembered it; no wonder Harrison had driven off so quickly.

"Interesting," said Neddy. "Now why do you suppose it's chained to the barn and not the house?"

"What d'you mean?"

"Most people have a guard dog to guard their house, not their barn. But I bet I could get to the house door quite easily." Skirting the edge of the yard – the dog by now was barking madly and pulling on the chain – he reached the door of the house. It was locked.

"Come back, you idiot," I said. "If that chain breaks, then you're Pedigree Chum."

He came back. "See what I mean? The dog isn't protecting the house at all. He's guarding the door of the barn. There's a padlock on it, too... What's inside?"

From the yard we could see right into one part of the building, where big double doors stood open. It looked as if it had once been a tractor shed. There were other doors around the yard, most of them bolted shut. But only one door had a brand new padlock on it and a guard dog beside it.

"Maybe there's a window round the other side," I said, and went to see. No luck. The back and side of the barn were as blank as a cliff-face.

"There's no way in from the side or the back. But what about from above?" For once I was ahead of Neddy. (I have cousins who live on a farm.) I showed him the little door, high up on the wall of the barn, which probably led to a hay-loft. And hay-lofts often have a trap-door leading to the room below.

"It's worth a try," said Neddy. "I think I saw a ladder at the back of the tractor shed..."

Now the dog was absolutely frantic. As we edged into the tractor shed, it lunged at us again and again, half-strangling itself on the chain every time. The noise it made was appalling. (At least it proved there was nobody at home.)

We had to set the ladder up below the hay-loft door, which meant we were within a metre of the dog's raving jaws. Trying not to flinch every time it leaped forwards, I climbed up. The ladder was old, with a broken rung, but I made it. One push and the door swung open.

The loft was quite bare apart from a few abandoned hay-bales at the far end. My heart sank; there was no sign of a trap-door. Unless it was hidden under the bales...

I lifted them aside, coughing at the dust that rose up. And there was the trap-door, bolted shut. Cautiously I opened it and looked down.

Below me was what had once been a cowshed or stable. It lay empty now, except for something wrapped in a blanket: a small figure, quite motionless, her hair spread out like a star on the dark stone floor.

Chapter 19

Hide

Finding her was the easy bit.

"How are we going to get her out?" I said. "We'll need another ladder."

There wasn't one. We decided to haul up the ladder we had used before, and lower it through the trap-door. It was very heavy; there was a terrible moment when it nearly slipped away from us to crash down on top of Katie.

At last it was in position and I climbed down. Now came the worst moment of all. Slowly I put out my hand to touch her...

It was okay. She felt warm to the touch, she was breathing. She was still alive! I began to breathe again myself.

"Katie. Katie! Wake up!"

She stirred a little and made a moaning noise.

"Katie. You've got to wake up. Come on – come on."

Her eyes opened. She coughed a couple of times, tried to sit up, and was sick.

"Come *on*, Katie. We haven't got much time. He could come back any minute..."

It seemed ages before she attempted to stand up. Instantly her legs gave way beneath her. She would never make it up the ladder, that was plain; I would have to carry her.

Trying to remember what firemen did on TV, I lifted her onto my shoulder. She was only little but she seemed to weigh a ton. I counted the steps of the ladder – twelve, with a gap at number five. Careful, now. Take it slow.

Half-way up I thought we would never make it, but I gritted my teeth and went on. I was sweating like a pig by the time I reached the top. We laid Katie down on the floor while we raised the ladder up again and lowered it out of the hay-loft door. Down below, the dog was leaping and barking like crazy.

"Don't you ever get tired?" I said to it. "Don't you ever stop for a tea break?"

By now Katie had revived a little. Her face was still as pale as the white-washed wall, but she sat up and started asking where she was.

"In a barn a few miles out of town. That man kidnapped you – don't you remember?"

"Oh! He put his hand over my face and something smelled funny, and then... that's all I remember..."

"Come on," said Neddy, "we haven't got time for this. If he comes back now, we're in serious trouble. Do you think you can climb down the ladder, Katie?"

"Course I can."

But when she looked out and saw the dog, she cringed away. "No! I'm not going down there! He'll kill me!"

"I'll carry you, then," I said.

"No! No! If you drop me he'll eat me alive!"

We looked at each other. Neddy said, "I'll tell you what – I'll go down and give the dog something else to think about."

He went quickly down the ladder and round the outside of the yard. The dog followed him, growling. When it had its back to us, Neddy began to tease it, stepping almost within its reach, then backing away. If it slipped its collar, the dog would rip him to shreds within seconds...

"Come on, Katie. Now's our chance. I'll go first – you follow me a couple of steps above." Maybe I could break her fall if she slipped.

Very slowly, a step at a time, she followed me down. I had just touched the ground when the dog suddenly realised what was happening. He shot towards us like a machine-gun bullet. Katie screamed and tried to climb up again – I grabbed her legs and pulled her off the ladder.

"There. Well done... you're safe now. Come on, let's get out of here."

We hurried her down the driveway and onto the road. Which way should we go? East or west, it was about the same distance around the Basin: two or three miles to where, beyond the mud-flats, the lights of the town were starting to come on.

"The bikes are that way," I said, pointing eastwards.

"Two bikes are no good for three people," said Neddy. "The nearest house is the other way – over the river. We could phone the police from there."

"How far is it?"

"A mile, mile and a half, maybe."

I wondered if Katie could walk that far. She still looked pale and shaky.

We turned right, and the road began its long curve towards the bridge where Ben had his accident. I wondered what on earth we would do if the kidnapper came back now. In the flat, open fields there was absolutely nowhere to hide...

Just as we got to the bridge I heard it: a car in the distance. It was on our road – it was coming closer. Its headlights glowed in the dusk.

"Quick!" said Neddy. "Over the fence and under the bridge!"

He was right; there was nowhere else to go. We swung Katie over the fence and leapt after her. The bridge was so low, we had to crouch underneath it with our feet in the cold, sluggish water. Katie was close beside me; I could feel her shivering.

The car roared over the bridge, and I said, "We probably needn't have bothered. I bet it wasn't him at all."

Neddy looked out cautiously. "We'll know if he turns off towards Saltmarsh House... which he's doing now."

"Oh-oh. He's bound to notice the ladder," I said. "He'll come after us..."

"W-w-will he set the dog on us?" said Katie.

"He will, if he has any brains," said Neddy. "Come on – we haven't got much time. Down the river. Hurry!"

"W-why down the river?"

"Water washes scent away – the dog won't be able to follow us. Oh come on!"

He set off in a sort of crouching run, keeping his head below the level of the river-bank. We followed him. The water was only knee-deep, but freezing cold.

The river ran out, wide and shallow, into the open mud-flats of the Basin, and I expected Neddy to change course. But he kept on running.

"Neddy!" I panted. "Stop! You can't run right across the Basin. It isn't safe – quicksand..."

"I know." Now he did swerve to the right, running parallel to the land. Our feet still splashed through shallow water – a long, thin lake between the mud-banks. After about two hundred metres he turned in towards the shore, and I saw what he was heading for: another bird hide. You could hardly see it in the gathering darkness.

We fell inside it, gasping for breath, our legs soaking wet, our shoes clogged with mud. Neddy shut the door and leaned against it. Katie sank down on a bench; through the darkness I could hear her ragged breathing.

"It's all right, Katie. It's all right. He won't find us here," I said, hoping it was true. If he did find us, how long could we fight him off? There was no way of locking the door or the window-shutters. Wooden walls might protect us against the dog's teeth, but what if the man had a gun?

In the distance I could hear the excited barking of the dog. It must be already on our trail, following it along the road to the bridge. What then? Would the river have washed away all trace of us?

"There's still the wind," whispered Neddy. His face was invisible in the darkness, but I could hear the fear in his voice. "I forgot about the wind. It's blowing from us to them... it will carry our scent."

Oh, help... I found that I was praying for the first time in my life.

Please, God – if you exist – help us. Don't let him track us down. If you really love us like a father, then please take care of us... even though we don't deserve it... even though we've totally ignored you until now...

It was useless. There was nobody there to hear. And now the dog was barking again, closer than before, and the man was shouting him on. "Good boy, Bruno! Seek them! Seek them!"

Outside, through a shutter that wouldn't quite close, I could see only blackness now. If the man didn't know about the hide, he would never notice it. But the dog didn't have to rely on its eyes. If the wind carried our scent towards it, our hiding place would be as obvious as if a searchlight was shining on us.

But wait a minute! The cold air that blew through the chinks in the walls – surely it was coming from the north now? From the land?

"Neddy," I breathed, "I think the wind's changed."

After a minute he said, "You're right. If only it stays in that direction..."

If only the wind did not shift again, it would carry our scent away from the land, far out across the Basin. If only...

Gusts of wind brought us the sound of the man's voice, sometimes near, sometimes farther away.

"What's he doing?" Katie whispered.

"He's probably going up and down both banks of the river," said Neddy, "trying to let the dog sniff out where we came ashore."

"But we didn't go ashore."

"Yes. Sooner or later he'll realise that."

It was sooner. The dog began to bark excitedly, and we heard the man's voice clearly. Judging by the direction, they were beyond the river mouth, where the mud-flats began.

"Good dog! Well done, Bruno! Now seek 'em. Seek 'em."

"It must have found something we dropped," Neddy muttered.

"Oh no! The binoculars! I had them when we left the yard and now they've gone," I whispered.

"Just shut up," Neddy breathed, "and stay quite still."

Which way would they go now? If they came along the shoreline towards us, we were doomed... But the sounds that came to us were from further away – further out over the mud. Soon, if they went on in that direction, the change of wind would carry our scent to them once more.

But something was happening. The dog's voice had altered. Instead of the deep, menacing bark, we could now hear a terrified yelping. It sounded like a frightened puppy. What was going on?

"Bruno! Sit. Stay. I'm coming," the man shouted. But then his voice also changed suddenly. He began to curse and swear; he sounded in a state of panic.

Cautiously I slid a window-shutter slightly open. At first there was nothing to see except the distant lights of the town, reflected on water where the tide was coming in.

Then I saw them: two dark shapes floundering in the mud. The man was in it over his knees, the dog up to its stomach. Every movement, every struggle, would suck them deeper in.

I began to laugh. "They've hit quicksand. They'll never get out of it, not without help."

The man had realised that by now. He was calling for help, but we could barely hear him. The wind took his voice and tossed it away, far over the empty mud-banks, into the night.

"Then are we safe now?" Katie asked in a timid voice.

"Yes. We're safe now."

Chapter 20

None the worse

I would have left him to drown, along with his dog. But Neddy insisted that we had to get help. So I found myself running once more along the route of the fun run, this time looking not for a checkpoint but for any house that showed a light. Forgetting all I'd ever told Ben about pacing yourself, I was in such a state that when I finally got there, I had no breath left to give my message.

The old lady who had answered the door looked rather shocked at the sight of me.

"What was that you said? I'm a bit deaf."

"Ring 999 – police – coastguard –" I croaked.

"But whatever's going on?"

I knew I could never explain. I could see the phone in the hallway behind her, so in desperation I pushed my way past her and picked it up.

"Young man! Look what you've done to my nice clean floor!" she cried, but I ignored her. I rang 999.

"Which emergency service do you need?" said the operator.

"All of them," I gasped. "Except maybe the fire brigade."

I wish I'd been there to see the rescue – but by that time we were safely back in town.

We heard later that they got to the man just in time. He had sunk waist-deep in the treacherous mud, and the tide was coming in. The rescuers, standing on firmer ground, threw him a line and managed to pull him clear, with the dog in his arms.

"He can't have been totally evil," said Ben. "He tried to save the dog's life, didn't he?"

"It wasn't worth saving – dirty great thing," I said.

Neddy said, "It was only doing the job it was trained for. I wonder what will happen to it while the man's in prison."

"Going to offer it a good home, are you?"

Neddy shuddered. "Not likely."

Ben said, "Will Paul go to prison for a long time?"

"Years and years," said Neddy. "Kidnapping is a serious offence."

"So Sarah and Katie won't need to hide any more," Ben said. "Do you think they'll decide to stay on here?"

I said, "I hope so. Katie's sick of moving around. And I'm sick of being a chambermaid."

"Mummy, mummy, I hate cleaning the bath... Shut up and keep licking," said Ben.

Neddy and I looked at each other despairingly. "Do you know," said Neddy, "we were starting to hope you'd grown out of that terrible habit."

"Why?" asked Ben, surprised.

"Your joke output seemed to have dropped lately."

Ben said, "With all that was happening, somehow I wasn't in the mood. But speaking of terrible habits, have you heard the one about the monk –"

Neddy and I made a hasty exit, covering our ears.

When term began again, Ben's leg had improved enough to let him come back to school. So he was there for the historic moment when the Head named the champion fund-raiser of the Fun Run. No, it wasn't Ben – he had raised his two hundred pounds, but someone else had brought in three times as much... Barn Simmons.

Barn stood on the stage in front of the whole school, grinning all over his big face, to receive his special gold certificate (personally signed by the Head). It was probably the only award he'd ever won in his life. Everybody clapped, most people cheered, and a few, such as Ben and me, stared in amazement.

"What happened?" we asked Darren later. "You said Barn and that lot were planning to keep most of their sponsor money. What changed his mind?"

"A polar bear," said Darren.

"Oh... Mr Wild, you mean. How?"

"Old Wild has a drink now and then at the Sun," said Darren. (The Sun is a pub run by Barn's dad.) "Before the race, he saw all the sponsors Barn was getting – pub customers mostly. Some of them were putting down stupid amounts like a fiver a mile. They didn't reckon Barn would do more than a hundred metres before he fell down in a heap.

"So then, when Barn only handed in one sponsor form and fifty quid, old Wild got suspicious. He had a quiet word with Barn's dad. He said, we don't want bad publicity for the Fun Run, so if Barn and his friends hand in all the money, we'll say no more about it. So they did."

"Just like that?"

"Just like that. You ever seen Barn's dad? He's

twice the size of Barn and three times as bad-tempered."

So it all ended well, apart from one person – Neddy. He's starting to go the same way as Ben.

"Not you as well," I said to him. " I never thought you'd end up getting all religious."

"I'm not," he said. "I'm simply keeping an open mind, that's all."

"But the way you always used to talk –"

"Ah. I have to admit, I used to be quite biassed. I didn't want to believe in God, so I listened to all the arguments against, and ignored the other evidence."

"What other evidence? There isn't any."

"Oh, come on, Jake. You were there. In that hide – don't tell me you didn't pray for help. I certainly did. And the wind changed, just when we needed it."

"So? It was pure chance. The wind often changes at nightfall."

"Possibly, but taken with all the other things... the way you remembered where you'd seen Paul... even the fact that you saw him in the first place. If you had-n't passed Saltmarsh House at just the right time dur-ing the Fun Run –"

"You're mad," I said.

He said, "You know what your problem is? You don't want to believe God exists, because if he does, you might have to change. You might have to do what God wants, not what you want. I know; I was the same."

"You're not going to persuade me." I said. "Why do religious people keep shoving their own beliefs down other people's throats?"

"I'm not trying to persuade you of anything," said Neddy, "except to keep an open mind. Don't you think it would be worth it? If there really *is* a God who loves us like a father, and if we can get to know him..." For a moment his face had the same wistful look I had seen in Katie, when she talked about finding her dad.

"I don't need another father," I said. "I have enough problems with the one I've got already." Because Dad had just appeared at the top of the steps. "Jake!" he called. "I need you to clear the tables. Get a move on!"

Whatever happens, the work must go on.

Katie seems to be none the worse for being kidnapped. (I suppose she was asleep during most of it.) They kept her in hospital overnight, then sent her home. A few days later her mum came out too.

Sarah still looks quite pale and tired. ("But then she always did," Henry muttered. "She's probably sickening for pneumonia or something right now.") It will be a while before she can work again full-time, but Mum promised to keep the job open for her, if she wants it. We have got a temporary replacement called Joel – an art student who is absolutely useless at the job. Even David would be better than him.

"Get rid of him!" Dad shouts when the Piggies complain about grubby bathrooms and unmade beds.

"Oh, I can't do that," says Mum. "He needs the money, or he'll be chucked out of college."

"This is a hotel we're trying to run, not a home for waifs and strays," Dad says. "I give up, I really do."

So if you're planning a holiday in Westhaven, my advice is, don't book in at Sea View. In fact, don't come to Westhaven at all. You'd have a much better time on the Costa del Sol – only don't tell Dad I said so.